D1395420

The
Mother's Tale

The
Mother's Tale

CAMILLA NOLI

First published in Great Britain in 2009 by Orion Books,
an imprint of The Orion Publishing Group Ltd
Orion House, 5 Upper Saint Martin's Lane
London WC2H 9EA

An Hachette UK Company

1 3 5 7 9 10 8 6 4 2

A CIP catalogue record for this book is
available from the British Library.

ISBN (Hardback) 978 1 4091 0158 1

Printed in Great Britain by Clays Ltd, St Ives plc

The Orion Publishing Group's policy is to use papers that are
natural, renewable and recyclable products and made from wood
grown in sustainable forests. The logging and manufacturing
processes are expected to conform to the environmental regulations
of the country of origin.

www.orionbooks.co.uk

For my husband and children,
without whom nothing else would matter.

ONE

It is early evening. I am suckling my infant son. We sit on the rocking chair in the nursery. Gently I rock backwards and forwards, pushing up and down with my toes. The lamp casts a golden glow over us. We are picture perfect, 'Madonna and Child in the Candlelight', a study for the old masters.

I look down at my son, at Zach. The small dimple on his temple works in and out with his efforts at drawing the milk from my body. His eyes are almost closed. I cradle my hand around his head; it is covered with a fuzz of hair, almost not human in its softness. I run my fingers over the dents in his skull, pleasantly concave to my touch. I press gently. They yield, a little.

I have always been fascinated by these unfinished areas on a baby's head. It is where they are most vulnerable, where the hard bone of childhood is yet to form. It is one of the reasons human infants must be tended so carefully and nurtured for so long.

What would happen if I press too hard, I wonder. What would happen if I took a skewer and broke the skin of his fontanelle, if I pushed it further until it met the soft resistance of my child's brain? If I continued pushing, would the steel cleave a pathway of immediate destruction and death, or would the results of its passage be more benign? Would the wound heal? Perhaps there would never be any obvious effect, or perhaps Zach would continue to grow for a time, until one day a mass of scar tissue pierced the trajectory of his development, keeping him forever looped in eternal childhood.

Even as I protect my baby so carefully, these are questions upon which I cannot help but ponder. It is the creative destructiveness of my motherhood; the alternating tide with which I wrestle.

Now Zach is almost sated. His sucking has slowed, but he is unwilling to relinquish the comfort of my breast. I insert my little finger between his lips and my nipple, carefully breaking the suction of his mouth. He pulls at the air in a desperate attempt to regain contact with my body, but then his head falls back. He is asleep. Breast milk, warmth and gentle rocking are powerful opiates.

I cradle Zach firmly to my body, rise to my feet and slip to the cot. Leaning over, I lie him gently on his side. One little fist rests on the sheet, the other is relaxed against his head. His skin is amber in the lamplight. I press my lips to his cheek, feeling the firm softness of very young flesh. In his sleep my child is archetypal, as am I, his mother and protector.

Tiptoeing, I move silently from the room. Closing the door behind me, I hold my breath and listen to the sounds of the house. From Cassie's room there is silence, from Zach's not a noise. Both children are asleep. I breathe again.

Remaining there a moment, I allow my pent-up energies to begin their dissipation. Sometimes at this hour I feel I might collapse, as if only the fast-forward movement of the day has kept me upright for so long. Now that I have an interval before the duties of the night begin, I am heavy and inert, a rag doll stuffed with lead.

I look at the clock in the hallway; it is seven-thirty, half an hour until Daniel arrives home from work. What will I do with this precious time? I decide to read. I made it to the library last week. 'A small victory for mothers everywhere,' I'd joked to Daniel.

But I ignore the books, piled so hopefully near the sofa. Instead I pick up the newspaper. When you are as tired as I am it is easier to focus on things in small bursts.

I try to turn the pages of the paper without rustling them. Rustling papers wake Cassie. There is a competition between the child and the written word for my attention. During the day I read standing at the kitchen bench. I turn the pages stealthily; occasionally I turn on the tap as though I am washing up. Then my daughter can't be sure what I am doing. In these small things, at least, I maintain some control, some power.

Tonight, I scan local politics and run my eye over the world news. All this is perfunctory, a prelude to the letters. I have always enjoyed the letters page. Once I was a frequent contributor. I enjoyed seeing my name in print; I could argue esoteric points with the best of them. Now I am an armchair intellectual; I observe from the sidelines as the regulars carry on their debates and trade their witty observations without me.

There's a discussion on child care being conducted in the letters page at the moment. Isn't there always? Those who have the time and energy, those without children, argue back and forth, quoting studies that invariably contradict each other.

We, Daniel and I, solved our domestic debate simply. I quit work. 'It won't be forever,' Daniel assured me, 'just until the children start school.' I agreed because I was too tired to argue. I have been too tired ever since. My views, my desires, my wishes have been silenced by exhaustion. I wear fatigue like a mantle; sometimes it settles over my head so tightly that I cannot think. Often I cannot finish sentences. My neurones stop mid-leap and I am left voiceless. My children have taken away my ability to speak. Thankfully they, my children, are sufficiently distracting that my lapses are rarely noticed.

Those with whom I now socialise are unlikely to care anyway. Those with whom I mix can be summed up with one word: 'mothers'. Once I knew no mothers, except my own desultory example of one. Once, if I met a full-time, stay-at-home mother I would not have known what to say to her. I would have devised an excuse to leave, to drink with someone else who was able to speak my kind of language. In those days my girlfriends and I were women who did things; who had fabulous jobs, successful businesses, rich boyfriends. We were witty and indestructible, a force with which to be reckoned. We worked, we exercised, we socialised – but most of all we had enough sleep to be able to function as rational human beings.

Now my regular social circle is a group of women who were herded together by the local early-childhood clinic for one reason only: our success at procreation. We cling together like jetsam thrown from a sinking ship. Perhaps I cling harder than most because the group provides the yardstick by which I can measure my behaviour. I am sometimes terribly afraid that without the group I would have no idea of how to be a mother at all.

The mothers' group met at my house today; there were five of us. That meant five toddlers, two babies, two pregnant mums and Rachael. Rachael is the one member of the group I do not like. She is a redhead, short and built hard, like a coiled spring. Her eyes penetrate; they see too much. Beneath her gaze I fumble; I am unsure. I dislike Rachael for the way she makes me feel, but deep down my reaction to her gaze makes me dislike myself more.

The group of mothers tries hard to be like larger society. We air-kiss, sometimes we discuss politics, we swap recipes. Often there are undercurrents of personality conflict, battles that nearly erupt and have to be smoothed over. There is much gossip and, apart from Rachael, a certain amount of mutual support. After all, most of us had no idea what we were taking on when we embarked on this motherhood business. Members of the group have even assumed roles of sorts: there is the organiser, the cook, the pessimist, the financial controller. We are a soap opera in miniature.

But always, in the midst of the intrigue and socialising, we are looking out for our children, to ensure they are safe, to ensure they will not be the child to first gouge out the eye of another. Our conversations are disjointed, our attention spans short: most of us are operating under conditions of extreme sleep deprivation. Not all of the mutterings make much sense. What a social study we would be!

'I've been trying to get Christopher off the dummy.'

'He's only one and a bit, Michael still has his. When he goes to bed anyway.'

'Yeah, I wouldn't mind that, but Christopher uses his all the time.'

'Yeah, Charlotte too. It's getting embarrassing. She's getting *big*.'

'Shit! Simon is into the CDs.'

Mad scuffling as a vain attempt is made to save the CD tower. Several minutes are spent collecting the CDs and removing them to my bedroom.

'Mind if I make another cup of tea?'

'Did you see the horrible accident last night, where the car was run over by the truck?'

'A truck! How many were killed? Charlotte, get away from that plant! No! Naughty girl!'

'Hey Odette, how come Jo couldn't make it?'

'Tamara's sick.'

'I saw them yesterday. She's bought a bike seat for Tamara and they go riding a lot. Jo's lost a heap of weight.'

'Really? It's ages since I've seen her.'

'Is it okay if I open the door for them to go outside?'

'Is she getting over her man ... What's his name?'

'Gavin?'

'Yeah, Gavin.'

'I think so, but it was a huge shock. Apparently he'd been having the affair all through her pregnancy.'

'Bastard!'

'I'd cut his dick off.'

'No way. I'd never allow myself to get that close to it again.'

'Get away from those rose bushes. You'll get scratched.'

'Who's for coffee and who wants tea? Jessica, can you pass me those cups?'

'I need another cup of coffee. I'm so tired I can barely keep my eyes open.'

'Tell you what, our sex life's been a shocker lately. It's like Simon knows when we want to do it and wakes up!'

'At least you feel like doing it. I don't have the energy anymore.'

'Me neither.'

'Sam bought me a black negligee thingy for my birthday. What a joke! It was two sizes too small. I told him to keep his fantasies to himself.'

'Hey, have you begun toilet training yet? Mum says I was done by now.'

And so it went on. I think I may have fallen asleep at one point. My head hit hard against the back of the sofa. It was lucky I didn't drop Zach.

Sometimes I yearn for an unbroken conversation: a conversation that is not centred around babies or husbands, or how tired we all are; a conversation that progresses somewhere in linear time instead of weaving and ducking around snotty kids; a conversation that has a purpose and an outcome. Now we talk to fill time, not to solve problems. We are people thrown together, who try desperately to have something in common besides our children.

Tonight I will attempt to complete a crossword. Once I was good at word puzzles, cryptic ones in particular. I always had a flair for language: an ability to make my point; a capacity for being noticed. My Year 6 teacher said I would go far. What is far, I wonder. Is this it?

TWO

A cry resonates down the corridor. It's Cassie. I look at the clock. She's been asleep exactly fifty minutes, one sleep cycle.

I hear Daniel's key scraping in the lock. I stand up, closing the paper as I do so, and open the door for him. A gust of chilly wind enters the house and in the glow of the outside light I can see spots of rain being blown around. Daniel pushes the door shut behind him and I reach up to give him a kiss. His clothes are cold, his face warm and slightly prickly.

'Will you try please?' I say.

'Okay.' He knows what I am asking.

I head to the toilet, but I am simply buying time. I am the only one Cassie will allow to settle her. It has been that way since she was born. Yet Daniel adores her and she him. On the weekends they spend hours playing together. Since Cassie's discovered the power of her legs she loves to run. Daniel chases and catches her and then tickles her tummy and her feet. Cassie relishes the attention from her father, but when it comes to sleep I am the only person she will allow near her. I know that it is simply part of her need to control me, but it doesn't make my lack of sleep and her constant demands any easier to cope with. It doesn't lessen the despair of what I have become.

As Daniel enters her room Cassie screams with all the power of her fourteen-month-old lungs. I hear Daniel's voice, low and controlled, trying to soothe her. He rarely loses his temper.

Cassie is still screaming as I wash my hands. I walk down the corridor to her room and tap Daniel on the shoulder. 'You go and warm up dinner. I'll be quick.'

Cassie's screams subside to a sob as I cuddle her. I squeeze, perhaps unnecessarily hard, and she gasps. I laugh quietly, 'Now you know Mummy's here.' I remember when I was young and had baby chicks to look after. I loved them so much that sometimes I wanted to squeeze them hard just to show them how much I *really* loved them. I worried about them excessively; sometimes I had dreams that I was too rough and broke their legs. They were such a responsibility, just like children.

Cassie kicks. She is not happy with my grip, not happy to go back to sleep, perhaps not happy at being asleep in the first place. Who knows? She needs to make her point. Her legs do it for her usually. They are expressive, powerful legs. They kick when she is happy or annoyed. They run when she wants her own way: to you or away from you. It all depends on what suits Cassie.

I remember the day Cassie first saw Zach in the hospital after I had given birth to him. She had not liked him – not the way he sucked at me, nor how I looked at him, nor how Daniel held him. The day that we brought Zach home from hospital, I put him on my bed to change him. I turned away for a moment and as I turned back Cassie's foot was coming down on his face. I wasn't quick enough. It was lucky, I think, that his bones had not yet hardened. Cassie received her first smack that day.

It was hard. Red welts rose between the fingermarks. I was sorry that I had to hit her, but it was the right thing to do. Now Zach was my responsibility as well, not just her.

Cassie grows heavy in my arms and her breathing deepens. Is it deep enough to put her down? Maybe. Sometimes we dance. I put her down, she screams. I pick her up again. It can go on for a while. Thankfully not tonight. I cover her and she rolls towards the wall with her arm around Scruffy. Her back is relaxed in the torpor of sleep.

I enter the kitchen; Daniel is heating dinner in the microwave. He has changed out of his work clothes and wears black track-pants and a white T-shirt. He is still nice-looking, I think. Still thin and tall. He jogs sometimes during his lunch-hour. I envy him the freedom of that time. I have no time to exercise and five baby-kilos cling to my hips and legs. Daniel says that they balance out my milk-laden breasts. I hate those as well.

We sit and begin to eat. Daniel chews slowly and carefully. He has always done this, no matter how hungry he may be. He is always the last at the table to complete his meal. I have seen waiters remove his plate, sure that he must be finished.

Sometimes, at dinner with other people, they've grown tired of waiting and ordered dessert before Daniel has finished his main course. He has never suffered from indigestion.

'Good?' I ask. I care what he thinks of my cooking now. Once I didn't. Once he was a better cook than I. Now I think he's forgotten how.

'Mmmmm, very nice.' Daniel nods and swallows. He knows my need. There are a lot of things about me that Daniel knows.

'How was your day?' he asks.

'Well, you know I had the marauding hordes. It was okay, but the house was a pigsty when they left. It took me nearly two hours to clean everything up. Luckily Cassie watched TV and Zach was so tired that he passed out.'

I need Daniel to know that I work hard while he is away. Sometimes I list the housework I have done: three loads of washing, cleaned the bath, scrubbed the toilet with my toothbrush. It is pathetic, I know. Daniel never seems to think so. He enjoys it when I talk. He enjoys talking as well.

I ask about his day. I do genuinely care. It is important that he is happy. Then I can be as well.

Office gossip is good from a distance. Daniel tells me the news from a recent sales conference.

'Samantha, you know Dirk's personal assistant, well she got together with one of the southern sales reps.'

'You mean slept together?' I ask. Daniel often speaks in euphemisms. I need clarity.

'Well, originally, yeah, but also just got together. She's leaving her husband.'

I search my mind for what I know about Samantha. 'Doesn't she have two kids?'

Daniel swallows. I see his Adam's apple working. 'Three.'

Three. That means stretch marks, flabby boobs, the works. I am amazed at her courage. It reflects the level of her desperation.

'So what about the kids?' I ask.

'I don't know. John didn't go into any details about them. I'm sure the kids are all right.'

Of course, I'm not really concerned about the children; what I want to know is if Samantha has made good her escape. I am sure that what Samantha has attempted is the effortless soar of an untethered bird. But I wonder, does she just have the new lover, or does she have the new lover and the old children?

Has the affair meant the beginning of a new life or the continuation of the same dreary old one, albeit with a different man?

'Find out for me, will you?'

Daniel nods, yes.

I can barely remember my own distant working life. I did it well though. I was one of the top account directors for my age in a major advertising agency. I had built and maintained an impressive client list – corporations that always insisted I be the one responsible for their new advertising campaigns. I thought I was unstoppable. That was until a missed period, a positive pregnancy test and a husband who was desperate for a child.

Now I have turned my efforts to being a perfect wife and mother, a gourmet cook, a spotless cleaner. I could chronicle what I am good at, write duty lists to show you what I can do. I know how important my work is. I know that without my labour the house would disintegrate, be buried under the weight of dirty laundry, the filth of unchanged nappies, the stench of accumulated garbage. This knowledge doesn't take away the tedium though, doesn't blur the frustrations.

On the days when I can laugh about it I invent new job descriptions for myself: 'defender against the chaos'; 'keeper of the order'. I once filled in the blank on a government form requesting my occupation with the description 'ordermaker'. Some data-entry person replaced it with 'homemaker'; the government has no sense of humour.

After Daniel has thoroughly masticated his last mouthful, we clean up. Daniel washes. I dry the dishes. There is companionship in this ritual. We have always done the washing-up together, from the first time I ever prepared dinner for him. It is one of the few things that has not been changed by marriage and children. I wanted to buy a dishwasher once, but Daniel said, 'No, leave it to me, leave it all until I come home. I'll do it for you.' And so I do leave it.

Following the washing-up we move to the couch to watch television. I lean against Daniel and he gently strokes my hand. He is very comfortable. I hear the thump of his heart under my ear. It is a calm heart, and strong. His chin brushes the top of my head.

After a while Daniel's hand slips to my breast. He works his fingers between the buttons of my top and gently pinches my nipples. I try not to push his hand away. My breasts are numb from Zach's tongue. They are functional attachments; they are not an erogenous zone.

Now Daniel leans over to kiss me, prising my lips apart with his tongue. I attempt to understand his desire. I know that he is not touched all day, not constantly pulled by the earthy demands of children who cannot have enough human contact.

Daniel flicks off the television and leads me down the hall. I know that he needs me, and through my fatigue I can clearly remember when I used to need him as well. Sometimes, after a good night's sleep, I can sense the longing again. And it is this longing that I miss the most, the breathless anticipation that sharpens and transforms the act which follows.

Daniel turns on his bedside light and I lie down, removing my clothes under the covers. I do not like my body anymore. Like an over-full bathtub it spills and tumbles wherever gravity is able to exert force. Two babies in just over twelve months have taken their toll.

A naked Daniel lies beside me and pulls down the covers. He rubs one hand against me, from my collarbone to my knee, from my knee to my collarbone. His fingers barely touch my skin; he resists touching my breasts or pubis. He is a musician tuning a fine instrument. After a while he turns me over and strokes my back in the same way. Small goosebumps of pleasure rise as his fingers travel smoothly up and down my bare flesh. There is a pause as he reaches into the cupboard for some oil. He drizzles it down my back and legs. I feel some trickle into the space between my buttocks and despite my tiredness I feel the wetness glide like a stealthy traitor between my legs.

Daniel refuses to hurry. He massages my shoulders, my spine, the back of my legs and knees. I feel lighter and longer as my muscles release. The fleeting desire has left me and now I simply enjoy the sensuous feel of his touch. I wonder if I will fall asleep like this, lulled by the warmth of his hands.

And then, Daniel runs one well-oiled finger down my spine, down my bottom and between my thighs. He slips it into me and the wonderful, the unexpected, desire returns, it frissons down my spine and I raise myself to meet his ministrations. As he continues to stroke, Daniel presses his penis against me. It is hot and hard like a rock that has lain in the midday sun. I am pleased that he wants me so strongly and the aphrodisiac of his desire builds my own. Very quickly, more quickly than I dared to hope, I am ready to come. Reading my body Daniel turns me over and pushes into me hard. He has timed his movements perfectly. He comes and in a few moments I follow. In the great rush of oxytocin that follows, milk spurts from my left breast, a white fountain of celebration that sprays Daniel and myself in its exuberance. I still haven't become used to my body bursting and leaking in ways beyond my control and I try to stem the renegade flow with my right hand. Daniel laughs at me and bends down to lick up the trickle that escapes from under my fingers before he collapses on top of me.

I laugh too. 'Holy shit! That was good.' I am being conservative. It was the best I have had for months, perhaps since the children were born. I feel as if I have been granted an unexpected, beautiful gift.

Daniel nods. 'It was good for me too. I love to see you like that.'

I roll from underneath him and kiss his forehead.

'Thanks. I love you so much, you know that?'

He nods. 'I know. I love you too. You know that?'

I nod. I wonder what I ever did to deserve this man.

THREE

We lie together. I am near oblivion. I am entitled to sleep tonight. Today, I have been a good mother, a good host, a good wife and a good fuck. What more could the world ask of me?

I begin to drift into the hazed world of sleep when Cassie screams. Daniel is snoring, so I ease myself out of bed. We tried letting Cassie cry once; it went on for nearly two hours. Daniel said never again, and I agreed. She likes to sleep with us and I used to let her, but now I often fall asleep with Zach in the bed and I worry about Cassie smothering him. I don't sleep very well in those circumstances. It is easier to attend to her.

Cassie is sitting up. Her face is red and blotchy. She is so distraught that she is having trouble breathing properly. She draws air in great quivery lungfuls and exhales in spurts broken up by her sobbing. Her hair sticks in tendrils to her forehead. I give her a cuddle. This time I am gentle. I don't have the strength to even attempt to assert my superiority. The sleep torture routine, which the children subject me to, is very effective in determining dominance.

It is a long time before Cassie can get her breathing back under control. I bring her a drink of water in a bottle and she sucks on it lying down as I push the hair from her still-flushed face. Her curls have begun to dry and I separate them with my fingers. The movement of my hand calms her and soon her eyes are following the up and down motion as I stroke her forehead. Her eyelids flutter and she loses the battle to keep them open.

I wonder what it was that caused Cassie to wake in such a state. Maybe she has had a bad dream. What nightmares do children her age have? Being left alone in the dark; becoming lost; travelling down the birth canal? Maybe it is the latter. Cassie's birth was long and hard. I remember it well, too well. I remember the pain, the unremitting pain. I remember how it tore, and thudded, it pulled and pushed, it pummelled. There was no part of my body that did not pulse with pain. There were cramps in my legs, spasms in my back, hammers in my head, a pulsating rock in my belly.

I remember how the pain stirred and swelled, heaved and peaked and then sucked back, taking parts of me as it went. I remember how the world, the building, the room, had shrunk to my pain. How its walls were as solid as brick; how I no longer had the energy to push through them or even against them. I remember the lack of control; there was me and pain and nothing else.

But even in the midst of this pain I knew that I had been betrayed. Nobody had warned me to expect this. Nobody had warned me that my mind and body would be sacrificed to a primitive hormonal force beyond my experience. Nobody had warned me that I would have no more control than a sick animal that lies panting in the mud.

I remember shivering in the shower that was now colder than the green bile which rose from my stomach and flowed around my toes.

I remember the nurse whispering to Daniel, 'I think we need to get her out of there.'

And Daniel asking, 'Can we give her something that will help?'

And the nurse replying, 'Gas, maybe, that's about it. She's close, too close for anything else. It might harm the baby.'

And then I can remember being angry. The *baby*, I thought! The baby was all right; I was protecting it with my body, it was encircled in the warm folds of my skin and tissue. For nine months I had been a human incubator while the parasite within fed from my blood, breathed from my air, sucked calcium from my bones and teeth, stole my mobility, my comfort, my identity. And now I was being told that the baby still needed to be protected while I was forced to bear this pain, this constant, dehumanising, unbearable pain.

I remember the need to push; my body being ripped in two; tissues tearing; a tic in my eye that wouldn't stop; my legs that shook with the force of supporting myself. I remember pushing and pushing again. I remember the unstoppable wave, the fundamental power.

I remember the tearing, hot pain of the head. The drop of shoulders and then the relief as another body slithered out of my own. It – *she*, I realised – slid into the hands of my husband, the arms of my husband. I remember the eyes of my husband examining this body, this creature to whom I had given birth. I remember him cuddling her, talking to her, warming her with his body. I remember that his eyes never left her.

I remember being alone on the bed, suddenly pain-free, shivering and bleeding. There was blood, so much blood. I remember the blood pooling on the floor down my leg. I remember my toes resting in it. I pictured a sponge being squeezed of its moisture until it was empty and shrivelled.

The nurse threw a blanket over my shoulders.

'There's so much blood,' I said.

'Yes dear, there always is. It's perfectly normal.'

Yes, I thought, *yes, there is always blood when something has been taken from you, when a sacrifice has been made. There is always blood when you've lost something.* I remember looking over at Daniel with our daughter. He still hadn't looked at me, and that was when the fear began to set in.

When, finally, Cassie was handed to me, I saw an ugly creature with a sloping forehead and flat nose and thought, *This could not possibly have come out of me.* I remember wanting someone to take her from me so that Daniel and I could go home together, so that we could forget that this had ever happened. I remember wanting to scream, *This is a mistake, a terrible horrible mistake that I never meant to happen.* But there were no screams, no one heard me and no one took her away.

When I had Cassie alone, I tested her reflexes. Her grip was surprisingly strong. Babies are like apes when they are born. Their hands are powerful enough to hold tight to a hairy underbelly. Their arms startle when they are dropped or scared, as if to cling to a tree branch.

I practised saying her name. 'Cassie, Cassie.' It sounded odd after months of referring to her as 'baby' or 'it'. The nurses were much more comfortable with it than I was. 'And how is little Cassie today?' 'Has Cassie had a bowel movement yet?' 'Cassie looks just like your husband.' I stared at her after this last comment. *No she doesn't. She resembles nothing more than a wrinkled prune.*

Cassie's face was slightly bruised; she had a small graze on her right cheek, caused by the pressure of her already long fingernails as she journeyed down the birth canal. She looked like a boxer who had been trounced. For a moment I felt sorry for her. Then she opened one eye and looked at me. *Look out,* that eye said, *for you will never be ready for what I am.* And you know what? I never have been.

In hospital I learned the mechanics of being a new mum. I learned how to change a nappy. I learned to bathe Cassie. I learned to hold my breath as my child's steel gums latched around my grazed nipples. But nothing had ever prepared me, nothing *could* ever prepare me for the mind-numbing tedium of it all, the torturing slowness of those first few days and weeks and months, the body and mind-sapping tiredness that meant I would sometimes fall asleep in the bath. Things have become easier since then, but I have never really become used to this new life.

I try hard not to reveal the extent of my anxiety. I am an actress playing a part for which everyone else knows the script except me. I search desperately for role models. Heaven knows my own mother never provided me with one. I follow Daniel's lead in parenting. I reference my actions to the members of my mothers' group. I believe that I am skilful in my deceptions. It is only myself whom I am unable to fool; only myself who understands the deep well of my fear.

FOUR

I stroke Cassie's forehead for a few more minutes before I decide she is fast enough asleep for me to be able to slip out. I enter the kitchen and make myself a cup of tea. I rest my head on my arm against the cup. The warmth of the tea is comforting.

I wake with a start fifteen minutes later. Zach is crying for a feed. Is it that time already? I feed him then wander to the lounge-room. Perhaps I shouldn't bother sleeping tonight. Once I suggested to Daniel that I move a mattress into Cassie's room so that she would settle when she saw me. He wouldn't hear of it. But he is not woken several times a night.

I am now too alert, too tense to be able to return to sleep easily, so I choose a novel from the pile near the sofa. It is *Love in the Time of Cholera* by Gabriel Garcia Márquez. I first read it when I was a student, but now my books are packed up. Our small house no longer has room for bookshelves. Zach's birth made sure of that.

Márquez's dense description fills the room. I have always loved the way he writes. In his books even the most mundane events become romantic. I wonder, if I could view my life from another angle, would it echo with the resonance of possibility and the capriciousness of fate, rather than with the dull thud of reality? Would I be able to view this time of child-rearing as simply a phase, simply another colourful weft in the tapestry of my days?

There have certainly been times when my life could have been fodder for fiction. Before I was a mother, *I lived*! I was a woman others envied and desired to emulate. I was influential in my work-life; successful in my personal relationships. I was a siren, able to lure men to my rocky shores.

Let me tell you how Daniel and I met. There are not many people who know the truth of it. It was at a gathering – someone's birthday, I think. I had come to the party alone, let down by a friend who had pulled out at the last minute. Apart from the host, I knew no one. Daniel was there with a woman. I can't remember her name. He was the centre of a group that I approached. I remember noticing how his hair flopped over his eyes and he kept having to push it back. I remember how he stood with his back to the sun and how, as he raised his head from his drink, his grey eyes met mine and I found myself caught in them, a small insect in an orbed web.

Daniel welcomed me into the circle. I glanced up and sideways at him. I could see that he was strong and steady. He looked as if he would be able to handle all that I am. I remembered my father; sometimes he had looked at me in the same way as Daniel had, as if I was the only creature in the world who truly mattered – supremely special. Daniel was the first man I had met since my father died who made me feel that way.

Later in the day, when Daniel's girlfriend was not around, I approached him again. He was sitting on a stone wall. I sat next to him. I found myself leaning towards him. I was a small metal filing experiencing the pull of the North Pole.

'Where is she?' I asked. It was a test: if he asked whom I meant there was no point in my going on.

'She went home with a headache,' he replied.

'Leaving you here at the mercy of all these women.' I was trying to be light, but my mouth was dry. I knew that I had a chance with him.

He laughed. 'Yes. It was brave of her.'

'Very,' I said.

He looked at me for a while, but I refused to look away. I knew what he didn't. When I want something, very little can stand in my way. And there was no doubt that I wanted this man.

I reached out one hand and ran it down the fuzz on his arm. He trembled, but didn't draw away.

'Perhaps I didn't realise just how brave she was being,' he said.

'Perhaps she knows how strong you are,' I replied.

'Strong.' He was not asking a question. He needed to fill the silence.

Gently I ran my fingertips between the webs of his fingers. Few people realise how sensitive these spots are.

He pushed down hard on the wall. The skin of his hand grew white.

'That's nice. No one's ever touched me there before.'

I laughed. 'You'll enjoy it more if you relax.'

'I can't relax here. Too many people know me, and her.'

I knew that I had him. I experienced a leap of triumphant power. I had tempted him away from another woman.

'My place isn't far away,' I whispered. I hadn't stopped rubbing and his body had begun to sway slightly.

He nodded.

We left the party separately, but rarely have we been separated since. It was as if we were never meant to be apart.

The night after Daniel and I decided to marry he presented me with a box.

'What's inside?' I asked.

'Open it,' he replied.

Slowly I opened the lid. The interior was lined with maroon velvet and inside was something that resembled a twisted figure of eight. I picked it up and turned it over. I could see that it had been made by joining together two pieces of broad, stiff tape. The tape had been given a half twist and linked so that it formed a unified structure. I had never seen anything like it.

'What is it?' I asked.

'It's a Möbius strip. Run your finger over the edge.'

Intrigued I did as he asked. The band had only one edge; I could run my finger over it for eternity.

'It has only one edge and one surface,' Daniel explained to me. 'That's what we are now, two people joined together to form one entity with a single purpose. I want you to keep it and to remember that's what we are now.'

Tears welled in my eyes. I had never been given anything so wonderful. 'Thank you,' I said. 'Thank you, thank you, thank you.'

As I moved over him that night I knew that no woman other than me would ever have him again.

I reckoned without Cassie, of course.

FIVE

oday is Saturday. I wake with Zach beside me, lying over my right arm. I don't remember bringing him into bed with us. Perhaps Daniel collected him at some stage.

Zach is dreaming. His mouth moves in and out, his eyelids flutter, his nose twitches. I watch him for a while. Babies' faces are endlessly fascinating.

As I try to ease my arm out from underneath him, Zach wakes. His face screws up, ready to call for attention. Both my children usually wake angry, enraged that some of their living time has been stolen from them. I've heard stories of babies who wake happy, content to lie or play in their cots while their parents exit sleep at their leisure. I am not convinced that such creatures exist.

Zach sees me and stops mid-bellow. His face contorts from a howl to a smile. He has forgotten that he was annoyed; now he gurgles and lifts his legs. His smile and eyes are flirtatious and warm. I tickle his toes, enjoying this moment of peace with my son.

I can hear Daniel in the kitchen with Cassie. They are making breakfast. Cassie is helping to mix the eggs. 'Round and round,' says Daniel. 'Faster, faster.' Daniel and Cassie are good friends.

While they finish cooking, I feed Zach. His red cheeks glow with stored fat. He is an eating machine. I will have to be careful when I start him on solid food. I don't intend for him to be a fat toddler.

When Zach and I enter the kitchen, Cassie is sitting in her highchair. Daniel puts a plate with small pieces of soft egg in front of her. He starts to feed her. Cassie doesn't much like her egg. Her legs twitch.

'Eat it, Cassie,' I say. 'Daddy cooked it for you specially. Yum, yum.'

Cassie pushes the first piece out with her tongue. Daniel inserts another morsel. This time Cassie's reaction is more dramatic. She spits it all over Daniel.

'Cassie!' I scream. 'That's not the right thing to do.' I feel myself turning red with anger. Cassie has always been extremely fussy with her food. It is another of her power plays.

Laughing, Daniel places one hand on my arm. 'Don't worry about it, sweetheart. She can just wait until she gets her next meal. Then she'll eat what's put in front of her. Won't you, Cassie?'

Cassie laughs at him lovingly. She has no idea what he is saying, of course, but Daniel is the centre of her universe.

While Daniel unstraps Cassie from her chair I put Zach in the baby rocker and sit at the table. Daniel has my coffee waiting, hot and milky the way I like it. I love the weekend. It is such a luxury to have someone else around to make breakfast and placate one of the children. My anxiety levels reduce dramatically.

Daniel leans over and gives me a kiss. He looks as if he slept well.

While he reads the paper I sip my coffee and eat the egg that Cassie rejected. She is fixedly watching television. As least she is not destroying anything.

After breakfast we dress the kids. Lots of layers, it's nearly winter. Then we head down to the park by the lake. We will have an early lunch while we're there, feed the ducks, push Cassie on the swing. Perhaps she will wear herself out and we will have a peaceful afternoon.

It is quiet at this hour. Fog-wraiths rise from the lake and dance for a moment before being burned off by the sun. Swatches of brown leaves cling stubbornly to spindly branches. The smell of wood-smoke tickles my nose, reminding me of a long-ago year in Europe when I rose early each morning to kindle the enormous fires of the hotel where I worked. Ducks on the lake move in slow motion until they see us, then their legs churn impatiently under the water to reach the lake's edge.

Cassie and Daniel scatter bread crusts, collected all week and carefully stored. Suddenly, man and infant are surrounded by ducks and moorhens. Zach and I are pushed outside the circle of hungry birds, but he has a good view from his position strapped to my chest and he squeals with delight at the raucous noise and movement. I squat, and Zach comes to rest against my legs, removing the pressure from my back. He is so happy that he begins to hiccup, especially when a curious duck comes over to see if we have anything to offer.

Two swans saunter out of the lake to join the melee. As if in the presence of Hollywood royalty, the duck crowd parts to let the swans through and they stand haughtily in front of my husband and daughter, demanding food. The swans' graceful necks rise over Cassie's head. She's had no experience with such massive creatures and she loops one arm through Daniel's legs. Tentatively, she offers a skerrick of dry crust to the biggest bird, but is too slow in the offer of another. The swan rears his head and hisses at her. The violent sound is harsh in the morning quiet. Cassie starts to cry and Zach's hiccuping stops with his sharp intake of breath. Daniel lets out a whoop of anger and surprise. I stifle my laughter.

Daniel reacts quickly to the swan's abuse. He scoops Cassie up, cradling her to his chest and shooing the birds away with his free hand. 'It's okay, honey,' he half sings to her. 'It's okay, they're gone.'

Daniel looks at me. 'Damn birds. Did you hear that?'

I nod. I wonder what it would be like to have a creature that size hiss at me: horrible, I imagine, but it was funny to see Cassie over-awed.

'Have you had enough feeding the ducks?' I ask Cassie. I have learned the hard way that distraction is the key to dealing with her. 'Let's go for a walk,' I suggest as I stand up.

Suddenly Cassie is okay. She wriggles out of Daniel's arms and runs ahead, kicking leaves and waving her arms at the ducks in imitation of Daniel.

'Do you want me to take Zach?' Daniel asks.

'No it's okay.' I am enjoying his solid weight against my chest and maybe carrying him will help burn a few extra calories.

Daniel and I link hands; his is warm and soft, mine cold and hard.

We walk fast. Cassie has trotted ahead and we are anxious to keep her in sight.

'Slow down,' I call. As usual she ignores me. She is bent on her own adventure; parents are an encumbrance.

As we round a garden bed I nearly collide with a woman. She is dressed in a dark grey leather coat and red scarf.

'Sorry,' I say. I am in a hurry to pass. I step left and she moves with me. I step right and she follows.

'It's you,' she says.

I look at her face. It is vaguely familiar.

'Don't you remember me? It's Maureen, Maureen O'Dowd. We went to school together at Cumberland.'

Daniel has moved ahead. He waves at me and indicates that he will chase Cassie. I motion him on. Now I have no excuse not to stop and talk to this woman who is demanding my attention.

I take one of her hands in mine. 'Of course I remember. You were captain of the hockey team. And the 100-metre record holder.' *Not much chance of that now*, I think to myself. She is quite fat.

'And you were a debating champion; your team won the state titles, didn't it? Do you keep in touch with any of them?'

I laugh. 'Oh no, there's a lot of water under that bridge. What about you?'

'Oh yes, I still have contact with quite a few people from school. It's good to have old friends, people that you shared things with growing up.'

I am still holding her hand. 'Well, it's certainly nice to see you again. What are you doing with yourself? I didn't even know you lived around here.'

'I haven't been here long, only a couple of months. I moved back here with my children. I'm recently divorced.'

'Oh Maureen,' I murmur. I give her hand a gentle squeeze. 'I'm sorry to hear that.' I can see now that she has been crying. Her eyes are red-rimmed and puffy.

'Do you need a tissue?' I pull a crumpled ball from my pocket and pass it to her. It gives me the excuse I need to let go of her hand. 'It's clean.'

'Thanks.' Maureen sniffs into the paper. 'But don't be too sorry. He was a real pig,' she sobs in earnest, 'but I don't know if that makes it better or worse.' Tears stream down her cheeks.

Oh God. I will have to hug her. I lean over and give her small butterfly pats on the back. The movement is very awkward with Zach between us and thankfully he soon begins to squirm. We pull apart.

'Thanks,' says Maureen. 'I needed that. And who's this?' She pulls at Zach's toes.

'Zach,' I reply. 'He's a bit over two months now.'

'He's adorable. Mine are with their father, every second weekend. With him and his new woman.'

She pulls out her wallet and shows me a photo of three rather ugly children ranging from about two to six. I mutter the appropriate compliments.

'I'm going back to school,' she says. 'I'm going to study accounting. As soon as Danni's at school

I'll get myself a good job. I'll show him I don't need him.'

I nod approvingly. 'Good on you. Never let the bastards get you down.' We both laugh. *Good luck*, I think to myself. Maureen is thirty-three, fat and unattractive, with three children. It is unlikely any man will want her again. She will have to raise three children alone. She will barely be able to keep them in order, let alone go to school herself.

'I'd love to catch up with you some time,' says Maureen. 'Can I get your number? And I'll give you mine.'

'Sure,' I say. 'Do you have a pen?'

Maureen rummages in her bag and produces a chewed pen and a torn envelope. She scribbles down her phone number and then hands the pen and paper to me.

'I really appreciate this,' she says. 'It will make such a difference to me to have a friend in the area. Especially someone like you.'

I finish writing and hand Maureen my phone number. It is fake, of course. I do not want Maureen crying on my doorstep when the grief and loneliness really set in.

By this time Zach has begun to kick impatiently. I use his agitation as an excuse to keep moving.

'It's been so lovely seeing you,' I say, 'but the natives are getting restless and I'd better go catch up with the other two. I didn't even have a chance to introduce you to them. Next time.' I lean forward and kiss her cheek. She smells of peaches.

'Bye,' Maureen calls. 'I'll keep in touch.'

I trot gently after Daniel. He and Cassie are crouching on the wooden bridge watching leaves sail downstream.

'Who was that?' he asks when I reach them.

'Just someone I went to school with,' I reply. 'Maureen O'Dowel or something.'

'Were you close at school?' he asks.

I try to remember. It is possible, yes. I remember sending notes to her once. I remember fancying her boyfriend in Year 10. I don't think he lasted long with her.

Daniel and Cassie drop some twigs in the water and then we walk again. The sun warms us. Zach's head comes to rest against my chest. The rhythm of my movement has put him to sleep. We stroll a little further and then turn around. If we go too far Cassie will need to be carried all the way back.

Our daughter is not happy at this about-turn. She pulls determinedly on Daniel's hand. 'More, more.' She learned that word very quickly.

Daniel hunkers down to her level. 'Time to go back, honey.'

'No! More!' Cassie pulls against Daniel with such force that her back is almost parallel with the ground.

'No.' Daniel is firm. 'It's time to go back.'

Cassie, too, is firm. 'No! More!'

'No, Cassie. What about the swings? Don't you want a go on the swings?'

Cassie relents for a second. The word 'swing' has resonated with her. She will consider this.

'No!' she decides. 'No! More!'

Daniel stands and sweeps Cassie into his arms. 'No more arguments. We're going back now.'

Cassie draws in her breath. This is the calm. The eruption will come. Her face reddens as she yells. She arches her back and kicks her legs. Daniel does not bother talking to her. It is all he can do to hold on. I start to walk. I don't want Zach to be woken by the din.

Daniel waits until Cassie realises that no matter how much she howls he will not release her and then he starts after me. I stop until they near. Cassie's bottom lip is heavy and her face blotched from crying. I am relieved that Daniel won the battle with her. Otherwise the next time would be even worse.

By the time we reach the playground Zach has become heavy and I ask Daniel to take him. I unstrap the pack and Zach wakes. He has on a red peaked cap that sits above his ears. He looks like a pixie. His eyes are grey, like Daniel's, not like mine. Neither of the children look like me. Lucky I gave birth to them, or I might be suspicious of their origin.

Cassie uses my freedom as an opportunity to pull me to the swings. I strap her in and push, higher and higher. I see her legs silhouetted against the sky. She looks as if she is catching white clouds with her feet. I wish I were able to swing again. I used to love going so high that I imagined I would swing right over the bar.

Suddenly, Cassie screams. I wonder what is wrong and then I realise that Daniel is calling to me.

'Too high, you're pushing her too high. Slow her down a bit.'

I reach for the chains and check the movement of the swing. I do it carefully, so that there is no jerk and Cassie will slow gradually.

'Sorry,' I murmur. I'm not sure to whom I'm apologising. Perhaps to the universe for the fact that I have failed to remember the extreme youthfulness of my child. Her personality is so strong that it is easy for me to forget that she is only fourteen months old.

Once Cassie has come to a stop I lean over and unstrap her. She reaches up to me; her face is wet with tears. She buries her head into the side of my neck where it is bare and she sobs quietly. It is unpleasant to have her cold, wet nose pressed so hard against me and it takes all of my resolve not to push her away.

Daniel pulls Cassie's toes. It is the distraction she needs. She wriggles to get down, and the three of them run. Zach bounces in Daniel's arms. His cap falls off and his fine hair lifts up and down in the air currents. Cassie giggles as Daniel tries to catch her and misses again and again.

I decide to begin the barbecue. Soon the sausages are sizzling and the onions are browning. Waves of heat rise from the plate. I breathe in the smell. It reminds me of a time before the children were born. Daniel brought me down here after I had won an important new client. The resulting international advertising campaign would bring millions of dollars of revenue to my firm. Daniel cooked sausages and opened champagne. I knew that he was proud of my work, of what I did and how I did it.

We also came to this park the afternoon I found out I was pregnant with Cassie. We sat on the water's edge eating fish and chips. That was before the nausea kicked in and I was unable to eat any food that had been cooked in oil.

We sat there for so long that day that the sun began to set. It was the end of the day and I felt as if it was the end of my life. Daniel, by contrast, was barely able to contain his exuberance. He had wanted children since we were married and ostensibly we had been trying to conceive for six months. But I had been secretly taking the contraceptive pill. As far as I was concerned Cassie was definitely not planned. If Daniel hadn't kept such a sharp eye on my cycles it is unlikely I would have gone through with the pregnancy. Cassie would not be here and I would not be what I am.

Today I look at the three of them running. Daniel was a good husband – *is* a good husband – only I share him now with two other people. On that fateful day at the lake we had agreed that once the baby was born I could do what I wanted – work or stay home. But after Cassie was born, Daniel made it clear that his real preference was for me to be at home. I did it for him, but, as I keep telling myself, this is only a phase in my life and phases don't last forever.

That night I have a dream.

I am in a pine forest. The fresh coldness of the air stings my nose and my feet slide on the needles. I am climbing – there is something or someone I must get to at the top – but I have a pack on my back and it is heavy, so heavy. I can't get the straps undone so I cut them with a knife. The pack rolls back down the slope and it begins to moan. Now it is a small black and white dog and it will fall off the mountain unless I save it. I lie down flat and try to reach it, but can't. I stand and inch downhill towards it. My feet slip from under me. I try to crawl but the dog slides further. I turn away from it. The dog moans more loudly, but I now know that it is him or me and the call of the mountain top has begun to drown out his cries.

SIX

One Wednesday night a few weeks later Daniel returns home from work very late. I have fallen asleep in the lounge-room waiting for him and I am woken by the feel of his lips on my cheek.

'Hello Sleeping Beauty.'

I wipe the tiredness from my eyes. I don't feel very beautiful. 'Hi, what time is it?'

'Nearly ten-thirty.'

'Oh God. It'll be time for Zach's feed soon. How come you're so late? You were strange on the phone when you told me not to wait up.'

'I've got some great news to tell you...but first, I have something for you.'

He reaches around into the hallway and hands me an arrangement of roses in a vase. It is an expensive vase, Wedgwood maybe.

'It's for being so beautiful, for being such a good mother, because I love you so much.'

'They're beautiful. Thanks, Daniel.' I reach up to give him a kiss. It is a nice surprise. He does not often bestow flowers upon me. Although I do wonder if he should have spent so much on the vase.

I put the flowers on the coffee table and we sit on the couch, clutching hands like lovesick teenagers.

'I'm glad you're up,' he says. 'I've got some great news. I don't think I could have waited until morning to tell you.'

'What?' I wonder what it could be. I have not seen him this excited for a long time.

'Well, you know how Ken's leaving?' I nod. Ken is the sales manager, a rather obnoxious man I've always thought. He was retiring, to tend his gardens or something equally ridiculous.

'Les has asked me to take his position.'

I let out a gasp. I know how much Daniel wanted this, but in our wildest dreams neither of us ever believed it would happen. Daniel's company rarely promotes internally at management level. We often joked that if Daniel wanted the sales manager's position he would have to leave the company first.

Daniel's hand is gripping mine so hard I can feel the pulse drumming in my fingertips.

'Do you know what this means, sweetheart?' he asks. 'More money, more responsibility. It means the company thinks a lot of my work, more than I ever expected. Les told me that they never wanted to lose me and that by promoting me they would be sure that I'd stay.'

'Oh, that's wonderful. They *should* want to keep you. I just never thought they'd be smart enough to realise it.' I rub his shoulder. 'I'm so proud of you.'

My words are right. I know that they are, but my head has begun to pound. I cannot stop the tears. Daniel wipes them away with his free hand.

'I knew that you'd be happy for me, for us. This will take so much pressure off us. We'll be able to pay off the mortgage much faster . . . you won't have to go back to work. We've both put a lot of effort into my career. It's finally beginning to pay off.'

Daniel is right: we have put effort, and money, into his career. He has recently completed a graduate diploma in business; it was a sacrifice of time, of money. And now he is successful. He will have more responsibility, more travel, more time away from home.

I look at the flowers he has given me and now I see them for what they really are – a present to his success, a present to his power and freedom. I begin to cry again. I am happy for him, I know that I am. But I also feel strangely empty as if something has gone from me. Or perhaps it never truly was a part of me.

SEVEN

*I*t is as I feared.

Over the next five weeks Daniel takes up his new duties in earnest. It is a busy time of the year, he tells me; it will not always be this hectic. But he is rarely home before eight o'clock and he leaves the house before six each morning. Some days he does not see the children at all. When he is home he is tired. He falls asleep in front of the television. I grow weary of reminding him to take out the garbage, to mow the lawn, and begin to do these chores myself. I am now a single mother with three people to care for. The knife-edge on which I walk is perilously sharp.

During these early weeks of Daniel's new responsibilities, Cassie senses my vulnerability. Her behaviour, already difficult, worsens. She acts as if everything I request of her is an imposition. For Daniel, however, she simpers and bows. If she is awake when he comes home he is greeted at the door like a conquering hero.

I now cannot dress Cassie without holding her down with one hand while pulling on her clothes with the other. She has discovered how to take off her nappies and she does so, often. While I am feeding Zach she will undress and urinate on the lounge-room floor. She is only sixteen months old, but she has complete bowel and bladder control, when it suits her. One morning she wakes, strips off and shits on her pillow. Daniel has gone to work when I find it, and her. She has climbed over the side of the cot, which we now keep lowered for her, and she is playing with some blocks as I follow my nose to the stench. It has obliterated most of the pink fairies that adorn her pillow slip. It has slithered down the back of the mattress and dripped on the floor. I am aghast and angry. I pick Cassie up and without thinking I rub her face into the mess. She gasps, gulps, inhales and bellows. For the first time in over three weeks I feel like laughing. She has no idea how small she is, how vulnerable. It is good to remind her.

Daniel tells me that he has to go away for three days. I can see that he is uneasy. He has never liked leaving us for any period of time. At his news I feel a chasm open at my feet. At the bottom are the monsters of insecurity, of fatigue and desperate boredom. I want to scream at him not to leave me. I want to bury my face in his chest and reveal that I will be unable to cope in his absence. I am shaking slightly as I give him a kiss.

'We'll miss you, but we'll manage,' I reassure him. Daniel appears to relax, his shoulders drop a little. If only it were that easy for me.

I write a list. We will keep very, very busy while Daniel is away. We will attend story time at the library on Monday, playgroup on Tuesday and visit friends on Wednesday. I will be so tired that by the dreaded dark of night I will fall into bed exhausted. I will keep the monsters away by the sheer force of my will and energy.

Monday comes and goes. I cope. I manage to get a few hours sleep that night. It is not enough, I know that, but it will have to do. It is all I have.

Early on Tuesday morning, before either of the children are awake, I make the mistake of looking at myself in the mirror. Was it three months ago I had that colour put in my hair? The regrowth is terrible. My eyes are puffy, with deep dark circles and crow's feet that run from their corners. I can't remember when I last put on make-up. I will do so today, I decide. It will lift my spirits. The ritual of mask-making will enable me to cope with the world.

I drag out my black make-up bag from the back corner of the vanity. I open the case. It is like looking at a lost world. Most of the products date from the days when I still worked, when I wore a different lipstick depending on my mood, the season, the colour of my hair. I have twenty shades of eyeshadow; my favourites are almost worn through to the metal canister below. I sift through the bag. I find some bronzing powder. I remember the exact occasion for which it was bought. It was a night cruise on the harbour. I dusted it over my – is décolletage the right word? – and over my shoulders. It was summer and the colour brought out my tan. I looked as if I had been touched by fairy dust. I knew that I was beautiful and so did Daniel. He couldn't keep his hands off me that night. I remember him rubbing against me as we danced. I pressed back; my nipples were hard with desire.

On the way home Daniel had unexpectedly turned down a side road and driven along it until it became dirt. There was almost no moon that night and when he had stopped the car and turned off the headlights the stars were liquid crystal pouring through the thick mantle of the night sky. The air was humid and redolent with the smell of the summer forest; it moved through my lungs as if I were breathing thick, sweet honey.

Without speaking Daniel moved round to my door, opened it and scooped me out in one movement. I rested one hand on his bicep. It was tight with the effort of lifting me. The back of my knees rested against his other arm. I was a current arced between his limbs.

Daniel placed me against a huge old tree. My feet were buried within its roots; my back rested against its trunk. I could feel the roughness of its bark through the flimsy material of my dress. My body resonated; it pulsed in rhythm with the earth. I stood before Daniel, an ancient sacrifice to the gods of the forest. His was the power, mine was the offering. But even as I stood compliantly before him I knew what I wanted. Never before had I desired a man so much.

Assuming the right of the victor, Daniel dispensed with preliminaries. He lifted my dress to my waist and pulled apart the lace of my underwear. I was exposed before him. He pressed his finger into me, up into my yielding flesh. And then he entered me. He was harder than I had ever felt him. 'Do you know that every man there tonight wanted you,' he whispered into my ear. 'And I'm the one who's got you.' He pushed into me again. 'You're mine.'

I reached backwards and held tightly to the tree for support. The heavens moved above me. The earth lived beneath my feet. As my gaze rested on the blue-black branches of the tree stretched out above us, Daniel came with a shudder of body and spirit that left him almost unable to stand. Quietly I laughed to myself. I know with great certainty that it is in the webs of desire that the real woman binds her man. Daniel might have thought that I was his, but that night I knew that he was mine.

Today, back in the dismal present, a cry echoes down the corridor. It is Cassie. She is awake and obviously not in a good mood. I put the bronzing powder back into the case. When was the last time men have desired me like that? Tears form in my eyes. I close the bag. I won't be bothering with make-up today after all.

Cassie lies listlessly in her bed and doesn't even raise herself to a sitting position as I enter. She is flushed and red blotches cover both cheeks. I feel her forehead. She is hot. As I bend over her, she coughs. It is a hollow cough that comes from the bottom of her lungs. *Shit!* The idea of spending the day at home with two children, one of them sick, is unbearable.

If I can reduce her temperature, then perhaps we will still be able to go to playgroup. I turn the heating down, wet a facecloth and place it on her forehead. I measure the appropriate dosage of paracetamol and, using a syringe, I shoot it down the back of her throat before she has time to protest. Cassie is not keen on taking medicine, although today she barely manages a murmur.

Now Zach bellows for me. I go and feed him and when I return to Cassie she is sitting up and taking more of an interest in the world. I feel her forehead again. She is a bit cooler. Will playgroup be okay or not? I prevaricate. Cassie is prone to exaggeration; she's probably not very sick at all. But then I wonder, what if she is really ill and something happens and I have done the wrong thing by taking her out?

I am shaky with the effort of thinking. Once I made decisions about contracts worth millions of dollars; now I do not know what to do with a sick child.

The phone rings. As I run to answer it Zach protests at being left alone for so long; I snatch him up as I go.

It is Daniel. He is calling us from breakfast. I can hear the genteel clinking of cutlery in the hotel dining room. He sips his coffee as he talks to me. He had a successful day yesterday. It's very warm there. He might be able to get home a bit earlier tomorrow.

I respond to him as best I can, but my mind is still on Cassie. Should I ask Daniel's advice? I want to and I hate that I feel like this. I hate that I can't make decisions about my children without feeling that I need to seek someone else's counsel.

Cassie toddles into the kitchen and wipes her nose against the back of my leg. Zach is trying to grab the telephone cord. I pull it as far from his reach as I can. Thwarted in his efforts he lurches for my hair instead and holds on with the desperation of a drowning sailor.

'Hang on, Daniel, will you?'

I forcibly remove Zach's hand from my tortured tresses, grab a tissue from the top of the microwave and wipe Cassie's nose. As I do so I notice that we are out of bread. Fuck! Two over-ripe bananas nestle forlornly in the fruit bowl. I know that we have no cereal. Looks as if breakfast will be a non-event.

When I return to Daniel he has begun on his toast. My stomach rumbles. I have two children to take care of and he is having his breakfast hand-fed to him. I will not ask Daniel what to do about Cassie. I will make this decision alone. We will go to playgroup and Cassie will bloody well enjoy it.

Playgroup is a disaster. The first person I see when I walk in is Rachael, from my mothers' group. She's never been to this playgroup before, so what the hell is she doing here now? She has come to spy on me, to make her snide comments, her rude remarks, to try to reveal my inadequacies as a mother. She is sitting on the floor playing with her child, and she nods to me, smiling, revealing her perfect white canine teeth. I murmur hello, but do not walk over to where she is sitting. I do not want her here, and I realise that if she continues to come I will have to find another playgroup. Fuck, another irritant in an already awful day.

No one is able to play outside. A cold easterly wind has begun to blow and it looks as if it might even snow. For most of the time Cassie sits listlessly on my lap. Her breathing is ragged and she only rouses herself occasionally in order to cough that same echoey cough. Zach is also restless and I try to rock his pram with one free hand. My coffee grows cold in front of me until someone takes it away to wash up. I still haven't had breakfast and my stomach cramps in protest.

Towards the end of the session, Cassie begins to burn up. Rachael walks over and places her hand on Cassie's forehead. She points to a rash on the side of Cassie's neck. 'You need to take her to a doctor,' she says. 'One of the signs of meningococcal disease is a rash like that. I can take care of Zach for a while if it makes it easier for you.'

I resist the temptation to pull Cassie away from Rachael's assured hand. 'No, thank you,' I reply. 'I can cope perfectly well.'

By this stage I am fuming. How dare Rachael, or anybody else for that matter, tell me what I should do. I am the girl's mother, after all. I will decide what is best for her. I attempt to shoot another dose of paracetamol down her throat. She spits it all over me. *You little bitch*, I think to myself. Cassie is determined to ruin my day and I am just as determined that she will not.

After playgroup I decide to call in to the shops and get some bread. I need at least that in order to get through the rest of today and tomorrow. When we arrive at the shops, however, both Zach and Cassie have fallen asleep in the back of the car. They have done it to spite me. A rage starts to burn.

I cannot leave the children in the car. This car park is patrolled by police and the fine for leaving children unattended in a car is high. I need this fucking bread. I will have to wake them and take them with me.

I wake Cassie first. She looks shocking, her eyes are bright and her face is even more flushed than before. I tell her to stand on the footpath and wait for me. Gently I ease the straps away from Zach's shoulders. If I am careful I might be able to carry him into the shop without waking him. I move his arms through the straps. He is still asleep. It is only as I lift him to my shoulder that he wakes and raises his head. I push his head down against my shoulder. If I can get him to keep it there maybe he will fall asleep again.

I take Cassie's hand; she pulls it away. I grab it again; she rips her hand out of mine and puts it behind her back. Being ill has not made her any less defiant. I grit my teeth and squat down to her level. 'Take my hand.' The words spit out of my mouth.

'No,' she says.

I hesitate, and we both know that she has won. A tiny child, flushed with fever, has got the better of me. Zach's head is bobbing around; he is well and truly awake. He starts a gentle keening. I turn my back on Cassie and enter the shop; she trails about ten paces behind. She is too short to set off the sensor that opens the door and she looks as if she will be crushed in its metal mouth. I take a step back to reopen the door and she moves backwards as well, still outside. If this weren't happening to me it could perhaps be funny.

'Cassie, come inside darling. The door will close on you otherwise.' I use the voice I save for when I am with my children around other people. It is the voice of a strong, calm, reasoned adult who expects her word to be obeyed. I move away again. I will not look at her. I won't. If I look she has won, again. As I move with bridal slowness down the aisle, I imagine her running into the car park and being squashed by a reversing car. I imagine a man walking past, putting her under his arm and running. But I will not look, or I will never be able to get this bread.

Cassie screams; the door is closing on her. It will open as soon as it touches her, of course, but she doesn't know this. I hurry back to her; Zach bobs around and dribbles down the back of my shirt. His keening becomes louder. The checkout ladies are looking at me. I am sure that the one with the steel-grey perm clicks her tongue. *Tsk, tsk, what a terrible mother, can't even control her own children.* I grab Cassie's hand; she has lost her opportunity for gentleness from me. She comes, pulling slightly, like a sail caught in a mild breeze.

The bread is at the back of the shop. We drift past some lollipops; a tactical mistake. The mild breeze becomes a gale. Zach and I are caught in the force of Cassie's longing. She has not eaten all day, but now she has seen what she wants. 'Lolly, lolly.' I reach over and get a red one. Her feet stamp. I put the red one back, get a green one and rip it open with my teeth. I will pay for it later; now I just want to be free to get the bloody bread.

I hear a sharp intake of breath as I hand Cassie the sweet. Belatedly I realise that she wanted to open it herself. But I have had enough. I leave her there to bellow, to drop the lollipop in protest. I trot to the bread stand, grab a couple of loaves and trot back to Cassie. I put the bread under my arm and seize her hand, half-dragging and half-carrying her to the checkout at the front of the shop.

Letting go of Cassie's hand I plonk the armpit-squashed bread on the counter. 'And there is a lollipop on the floor. I'm afraid I opened it and my daughter didn't want it. I'll pay for it, of course, but I wanted to let you know that it's there.'

Steel-grey perm shakes her head. 'Which aisle?'

'I don't know. The lollipop aisle?' Humour attempted.

Steel-grey perm shakes her head again. Humour rejected.

Cassie has collapsed in a dramatic heap on the floor, her head is under the counter and she is bellowing for all she is worth. Zach wails in harmony with her. Suddenly Cassie stops. I breathe a sigh of relief – one down. And then I wonder what Cassie has found. I can imagine her scraping up some forgotten chewing gum and ingesting it. I try not to gag.

The bread is bagged. This ordeal is nearly over – or so I dare to hope. 'Come on Cassie, time to go.' The little feet with their red shoes and frilly socks do not move.

I step over her. 'Come on.' I attempt my reasoned, not to be argued with voice, but the quaver at the end belies my assumed confidence. I reach down and pull her out; using her bottom as a pivot I spin her around to face me and pull her up by one arm.

It is quick; she is too shocked to protest. I have the bread bag dangling from the hand with which I am holding Zach. My bicep feels as if it will burst. I drag Cassie towards the door. Steel-grey perm turns to the other shop assistant. 'When my children were that age I never went shopping with them.' I swallow my vitriol. She is hardly worth it, but I will not be shopping here again.

I deposit Zach in the car. His face is blotchy from crying, but he likes the car and I know that he will soon settle. Cassie arches her back as I try to strap her in, and she starts screaming. I have had as much as I can take. Quickly I look around to check that no one is watching. Then I give Cassie a hard slap on the face. By now her cheeks are so red from fever and crying that my fingermarks cannot even be seen.

EIGHT

When we arrive at the top of the steep driveway of our house I see that the garage door is open and Daniel's car is parked inside. As I pull up behind him I feel relief wash over me. I am glad now that I made the decision to stop and buy the bread. Daniel likes to have bread with his meals.

Both of the children are asleep again and I leave them in the car as I greet Daniel, who has come out to see me. We hug for several heartbeats and then he pushes me back to face him, kissing my mouth, my nose, my eyes. I laugh. His lips tickle, his breath is coffee-laden. I burrow my head in between his jacket and his armpit. I can smell his sweat; it is sweet and cloying, like a tropical carnivorous flower.

'How come you're back so early?' I ask.

'Things were cancelled. Not long after I spoke to you. There was nothing to keep me there so I caught the first available plane. I tried to call you a few times but there was no answer.'

'We were at playgroup. It was dreadful. Cassie whinged and whined the whole time. I didn't get to drink my coffee and I haven't had breakfast yet, let alone lunch.'

'Come on then. Let's get the kids into the house and we can make something to eat.'

Daniel walks around to Cassie's side of the car and as he lifts her from her seat he exclaims, 'My God, she's burning up. Has she been like this for long?'

'She was warm this morning,' I reply. 'But I got some paracetamol into her and she seemed all right. She spat the last dose out so I suppose that's why she's a bit warm now.'

'A bit warm! She feels as if she's on fire. You went out with her like this, in this weather?' He sees the bread. 'And you went shopping?'

I nod. 'Yes, but she wasn't this bad when I left home and I needed bread.'

I can see that Daniel is reluctant to say any more, but of course he has said enough. I have been judged and found wanting.

'Don't take Zach out of the car,' he says. 'I think we should take her to the doctor. Did you see this?' Gently he lifts Cassie's chin. Underneath, the rash is now burning bright red. 'One of the symptoms of meningococcal disease is a rash.'

And Daniel, like Rachael, obviously believes that I have failed to notice a rash on my own daughter. Do they both think that I am completely incompetent?

We get into the car and head to the 24-hour medical centre, which is unusually quiet; we are led through to a doctor in record time. Perhaps the fact that Cassie is lying listlessly in Daniel's arms helps.

The doctor examines Cassie carefully.

'How long has she been like this?' she asks.

'She was a bit warm when she woke this morning,' I reply. 'But she only really started to burn up around lunchtime.' That was my story and I was sticking to it.

'It's lucky that you brought her in,' says the doctor. 'I know that you've been focusing on the rash, but that's not actually what I'm worried about. Your daughter has fluid on the lungs, a lot of fluid in fact. I think she has bacterial pneumonia. Another day without treatment and she may have required hospitalisation.'

Daniel looks at me. I know that I have failed.

'So what now, Doctor?' Daniel asks.

'I'm going to prescribe some antibiotics. It's important that you keep her warm and maintain her fluids. It's also probably better if you don't take her out anywhere, particularly in this weather. I'll need to see her again in a few days to check that the antibiotics have kicked in. But you should bring her in earlier if she takes a turn for the worse.'

With our instructions and our antibiotics we return home. It is almost two-thirty and I still have not had anything to eat.

Daniel carries Cassie inside. He lies her on the couch while he makes up a mattress in front of the television. Then they lie down together watching a children's program. Daniel strokes her hair in an almost absentminded way.

'Don't worry baby, Daddy's here now. You'll be all right now.'

Baby snuggles in against Daddy's chest. I can see the tops of their heads, but I have been excluded from the circle of their mutual affection. I turn away. I will continue with the task of settling Zach. At least he will be happy to be with me. For a second I allow myself the thought that maybe it was a pity Daniel returned home early.

NINE

Cassie bounces back with a vengeance in the weeks following her pneumonia. It is as if the antibiotics have given her even more stamina and greater defiance. She runs me ragged. Daniel frequently comes home from work a little earlier now, but I do not flatter myself that it is because of me. It is Cassie whom he kisses first, Cassie for whom he buys little gifts. Now I wait in line to see if there is any affection left over. Sometimes there is, sometimes there is not.

I am beyond exhaustion. I am beyond expectation. I am beyond hope. I can see nothing but my own fear and fatigue and self-loathing stretching before me for a lifetime. I feel as if there is nothing left.

Tonight Cassie is calling for water. As usual Daniel snores through the noise. His greater solicitude towards his daughter has done nothing to cure his nocturnal deafness. I am still the one woken by the children several times a night. I am the zombie who cooks their meals; I am the maid who cleans their shit.

Now Cassie is screaming. I fill a bottle and take it in to her. She sucks at it lying down; her eyes are still closed, eyes that look nothing like mine. Her eyelids are purplish; I can almost see the blood moving within them. She looks so small and vulnerable, but I know the strength of her will. It frightens me; perhaps I will always be a slave to that will, to the power of her kicking legs.

I see a future where Cassie and I continually clash – and Daniel may not choose to take my side. I see a future where I will be excluded from their favour, from Daniel's favour. I see a future where this period of my life is not a phase and will not pass.

Cassie finishes her drink and lets the bottle fall to the floor. I pick it up and put it on the night stand. She rolls around and grumbles about something. She wriggles and squirms as if she cannot become comfortable. Her breathing is growing heavy, but she is having trouble settling.

'Shhh, Cassie, shhhh,' I whisper. 'Time to go back to sleep.'

Cassie grumbles a bit more. She has never liked to do as I ask.

I pull a pillow from the rocking chair. It might make things more comfortable for her. It is a small pillow, not much bigger than her face. I put it close to her in order to better compare its size. I see that the pillow covers her whole head. I hold it against her face gently and then more firmly. Her legs begin to kick. She fights against me as if she expects me to give in to her as I usually do. But this time I don't.

After she has been still for some time I take the pillow away and replace it on the rocking chair. Cassie's mouth is open a little. No breath comes out.

I have told her many times that she must listen to me.

I return to bed. I hope that Zach sleeps through the rest of the night.

TEN

*D*aniel's screaming wakes me. He is surprisingly loud. *What is he doing?* I wonder; *he will wake Zach.* Then I remember.

I rise from bed and put on a dressing-gown. By this stage Daniel is almost hysterical.

'Call an ambulance, Cassie's not breathing.'

I hurry down the corridor to her room. I see Daniel's back. He has placed Cassie on the floor and is crouching over her, breathing into her lungs. *Exhale, turn head, inhale.* I remember learning the action at Girl Guides. With a child as young as Cassie there is no need to hold the nose when blowing into the lungs. An adult's mouth is large enough to place over both the nasal and mouth cavities. This is what Daniel is doing now.

I move into the room and step around Daniel. Cassie looks so tiny lying there on the floor. I reach down and touch her toe. It is very cold.

'Will you call an ambulance!' yells Daniel. I jump at the urgency in his voice. As I leave the room, Daniel starts CPR.

I reach the phone and dial 000.

'Ambulance. We have a child, seventeen months, not breathing.' I pause. 'She is very cold.'

The voice on the other end is detached and professional. It asks my address.

'Tyson Avenue. Number fifteen.'

The voice gives instructions on emergency measures to try before the ambulance arrives. I reply that Daniel is already giving Cassie CPR, but that she is cold, very cold.

The voice tells me that the ambulance will be there in a matter of minutes, that I can hang up now, but to stay calm, help is on its way.

Zach has been crying for some time. I enter his room. He greets me with a smile. I pick him up. He is so warm. I feel his breath against my cheek. I hold him to me. There is nothing I can do to help Daniel and I am enjoying the warmth of Zach's young body.

There is a sharp rap on the front door. It is the paramedics. They were quick, I think, as I open the door. It is a man and a woman, both dressed in black pants and white jumpers, like penguins. I direct them to Cassie's room. The woman enters first. She touches Daniel's shoulder and asks him to move away from Cassie's body. Daniel doesn't want to give her up to them. He hovers and circles, like a search plane. I can see that Daniel is in the way of the paramedics so I go up to him and pull him out of the room, away from Cassie, into the corridor with Zach and me.

I cradle Daniel in one arm and Zach in the other while the ambulance officers look after Cassie. It is a relief to have her in professional hands. Daniel and I cry. I join him in his rhythm. Only Zach is happy. He dribbles on my hand.

Daniel travels in the ambulance with the body of our daughter. The paramedics do not bother with the siren. It is obvious to everyone that it is too late for heroics and last-minute dashes.

Zach and I follow the ambulance to the hospital. The two previous times I have taken this trip at this hour I was in labour. The small bodies of my children were ready to begin life on their own. Now I am following the lifeless body of my daughter. It is the cycle of things, I tell myself. It is not what I would have expected – to lose a child before myself – but there it is.

By the time I find a parking spot at the hospital Daniel has disappeared with the paramedics and Cassie. I want to follow, but Zach is overdue for a feed and my breasts are aching with their load. I take myself to a small waiting room, sit in a quiet corner and close my eyes while Zach eats. Suck, suck, swallow. It is the rhythm of motherhood, the rhythm of my life.

Finally, Daniel joins me.

'She's gone,' he says. 'There's nothing anyone can do for her. Cassie's dead.'

I reach out one of my hands and clasp one of his. A terrible silence settles over us. It is broken only by the steady dripping of Daniel's tears.

We are led to the room where Cassie is lying. We are encouraged to pick her up, to hold her. I give Zach to Daniel in order to free my arms, but it is all I can do to run my fingers through Cassie's hair. It was washed last night and it slips through my fingers like quicksilver. I lift her hand and it falls back. My eyes feel as if the lids are coated in sand. I blink and tears form. Daniel takes my hand. Zach gurgles. He does not know the enormity of it all. I think that I am beginning to.

We are asked to wait in a large room clad almost entirely in linoleum; the material covers the floor and runs halfway up the walls. It is a dirty grey colour. The room is dreary and smells of antiseptic and old age. After a few minutes, a figure in a white coat enters the room. He shakes hands with Daniel, then me.

'My name is Doctor Hadid,' he says. 'I am terribly sorry for the tragedy which has befallen your family.'

He is softly spoken. Or perhaps he is simply respecting our need for quiet at a time like this.

Daniel chokes back a sob.

'We will all do everything we can to help you through this period. The hospital can put you in touch with grief counsellors, support groups.'

Daniel and I both nod. We know that everything will be inadequate, of course, but we can't refuse their offer of help.

As Doctor Hadid is talking a nurse enters and stands silently by the door.

The doctor continues. 'Right now we want to try to understand what may have happened to your daughter.' He motions us over to a small table in the corner of the room.

'We hope you will not mind answering a few questions. We understand it may be difficult, but it is important that we do this quickly while your memories are clear. You see, sudden, unexplained, infant death is not as common as people think, and at your daughter's age it is very unusual. What we are hoping is that you may be able to give us some clue as to why she died.'

'Yes,' says Daniel. 'Of course we will do everything we can to help.'

I concur quietly. I realise that what we are finding ourselves up against is a system that has to be seen to cross its t's and dot its i's. In the darkness of last night I had not paused to consider what might happen next. I now understand that things have not ended with Cassie's death. It seems as if they might be just beginning. My instinct has carried me this far, but I will need more than that to get me through this. I will need to be clear-headed and very, very careful.

We sit at the table and Doctor Hadid begins.

'Was Cassie her usual self last night when you put her to bed?'

Daniel looks at me. I nod. 'Yes. She always liked me to be the one to put her to sleep. She went down fairly easily last night.'

'She hadn't appeared sick…no temperature, no cough, no complaining of aches or pains?'

'Well,' I reply, 'she was only seventeen months old.' Doctor Hadid makes a note on his paper. 'She couldn't really tell me in detail if anything was wrong.'

'She had pneumonia a month or so ago.' Daniel breaks in. 'But she was prescribed antibiotics and was given a clean bill of health.'

Doctor Hadid is scribbling on his paper again. 'Really? How serious was the pneumonia?'

'Serious enough,' says Daniel. 'It developed extremely quickly, and the doctor told us that if we'd waited another twenty-four hours there was a good chance she would have had to be admitted to hospital.'

'Oh God, Doctor,' I say, 'you don't think that had anything to do with her death, do you?'

Doctor Hadid shakes his head. 'It's unlikely unless the symptoms recurred, and you say that she appeared well last night – not grizzly or off-colour at all?'

'Not that I noticed,' I say.

'I got home around eight o'clock and checked on Cassie then,' adds Daniel. 'She was asleep, but seemed absolutely fine.'

Doctor Hadid makes another note. 'Was Cassie in the habit of waking during the night?'

Daniel nods. 'Yes, she was becoming better at sleeping through, but most nights she still woke, she...wasn't a very good sleeper.' His voice wavers on the edge of tears.

'What about last night?'

'I didn't hear her,' says Daniel. 'But I was pretty tired.' He looks at me. 'What about you, sweetheart?'

'No, I have to admit I didn't hear her either. I did get up to Zach at about midnight. I didn't go into Cassie's room, because I didn't want to run the risk of waking her.'

'Did it worry you this morning that she hadn't woken?' Doctor Hadid looks at Daniel. 'I understand that you were the one who found her?'

'Yes, I was. This morning I really only checked her out of habit. As I said, she was beginning to sleep through the night and even if she did wake I didn't always hear her. But when I looked in on her this morning she wasn't breathing.' Daniel begins to cry again.

'Yes, I see,' says Doctor Hadid. His gaze rests on Daniel a little longer than seems necessary and I notice that the nurse hasn't moved. She has been quietly noting our reactions to Doctor Hadid's questions. *My God*, I think, *could it be that they suspect Daniel of having something to do with Cassie's death?* The thought seems ridiculous; I know that Daniel is an exemplary father, but of course these people know nothing about us, nothing at all.

Doctor Hadid turns to me. 'And how have you been since the birth of your children? Two babies born in such quick succession can be very taxing on the body, and the mind.'

How dare he! 'I have been perfectly well,' I reply. 'Tired, of course, but perfectly well.'

'I can vouch for that,' says Daniel. 'My wife has handled the birth and raising of our two children very...' he stops as he searches for the right word, 'well... As she handles all things.'

There are a few more questions from Doctor Hadid. And then, a statement. 'We would like your permission to perform an autopsy.' He looks at each of us in turn.

'It's standard procedure in cases like this, I'm afraid. From the information you have just given me, the cause of Cassie's death is not readily apparent and cannot be ascertained without an autopsy. Requesting your permission is a formality really.'

'So why ask us?' I am horrified, caught off-guard by the doctor's request. I realise now that it was stupid of me, but I never expected this. 'I mean surely it's clear what Cassie died of, Sudden Infant Death Syndrome! It's always in the news. Surely that's what she died of! What else could it be?' I am nearly hysterical by the last word.

Daniel grips my hand. We'll get through this, he seems to be saying.

'My wife is upset. Naturally the thought of our daughter being…interfered with in such a way is distasteful to us both, but, as you point out, we can do nothing but agree.'

'Thank you,' says Doctor Hadid. 'I know that this is terribly upsetting. Hopefully an autopsy will give us some indication as to what may have caused Cassie's death,' Doctor Hadid turns to face me, 'but, I would still like your blessing on this.'

What can I say? I utter the only words available to me. 'Yes, of course. If you think it is necessary. We will do everything we can to help.' I hope that I sound convincing. 'Can you tell us how long it will take?'

'About four days I expect. We will do everything we can to speed it up. We understand you will want to make funeral arrangements as soon as possible.'

Four days. I have four days in which I can do nothing, four days to wait while others decide my future. Only four days. They will be an eternity.

ELEVEN

We, the three of us, all that remains of our family, return home. Daniel drives as I am too overcome with emotion to handle the car. I sob uncontrollably into a handkerchief. To the world outside my head I am shattered-grief personified. But what only I know is that I cry for myself, I cry to cover my fear, for I am very afraid. I am afraid of what the doctors with their sharp scalpels and inquiring minds will find. I am afraid that they will have no respect for the family that Cassie's death has left behind. I am afraid that they will uncover what should be left hidden.

Daniel speaks. 'I hated leaving her there. I hated leaving her on that cold table surrounded by people she doesn't know.'

That is an understatement. I had to drag Daniel out of the hospital. Hadn't he been able to see that Cassie was dead? There was nothing, nothing either of us could do for her. Now it is time to get on with the lives of the three of us who remain.

I begin to sob even harder.

Daniel reaches out with his spare hand. He doesn't speak. I don't think that he trusts himself to.

When we arrive home I am shocked to see a police car parked out the front.

'What are they doing here?' I ask Daniel. I expect him to reply that he doesn't know. Instead his answer surprises me.

'It seems that a death-scene investigation, as well as an autopsy, is par for the course in a situation like this,' he says dryly. Obviously he also is not impressed with the level of bureaucracy that's slammed into our lives as a result of the death of our daughter. 'I gave them the key while we were at the hospital. Apparently they need to do it as soon as possible. I wanted to get it over and done with. I hope you don't mind.'

I shake my head as fear runs through me. I know that Daniel has done the right thing, that in his shoes I would have acted as he did, but I feel betrayed by his actions. The problem is that in the cold, numb emotion of last night I had not considered scenes such as these. I am unprepared. I cannot be sure that everything in the house is as it should be.

A uniformed female police officer comes out to greet us as I am taking Zach from the baby capsule. She introduces herself as Senior Constable Coombs.

'I'm so very sorry about what happened here this morning,' she says. She succeeds in sounding genuine in her concern even though this is simply another job for her. 'Thanks for being so good about letting us in. Families find things like this really hard, but it helps everyone if we can get in and get it all over with.'

'Have you finished yet?' Daniel asks. He is using his professional voice. I know that he is trying hard not to crumble.

'Almost, sir. We just have a few questions. If you both wouldn't mind...?'

'No!' Daniel almost barks. With difficulty he manages to modulate his voice. 'No, we don't mind. Let's get this over with.'

Senior Constable Coombs shows us into our own lounge-room. We make ourselves comfortable, but the scene is all wrong. I could never have imagined that my life, our life, would come to this.

Another officer enters the room and Coombs clears her throat. 'Ummm, I'm sorry, but it's standard procedure in a case like this for us to speak to the parents separately.' She gestures towards Daniel. 'Sir, could I ask you to accompany Constable Stanley? He will speak to you in the kitchen.'

'No,' says Daniel. 'No! I'm not happy about this. Can't you see the state my wife is in? She's absolutely distraught. We've been through so much already today.'

'I understand how difficult this is, sir,' replies Coombs, 'but these are only routine questions that must be asked. There is nothing to be alarmed about. It will all be over in a few moments. Please, sir, if you would accompany Constable Stanley we will be out of here in less than half an hour.'

Daniel hesitates. He looks at me. I nod slightly. It is better, I think, if we get this over with. I will gather my reserves. I will answer their questions. Since when has some half-educated policewoman been any match for someone like me?

As soon as Daniel leaves the room with Zach Coombs begins her questioning. They are what I imagine to be largely standard. What time did Cassie go to bed last night? What did she eat? Did she wake? Was she well? Who was in the habit of putting her to bed? You've watched enough police dramas to know the score.

I really can't remember all the questions. The to-ing and fro-ing is strangely melodic. Some of my fear has begun to abate and I have almost slipped into a trance when Coombs unwittingly drops a bombshell. 'We noticed there was an empty water bottle near Cassie's cot. Can you tell me who put that there and when?'

The water bottle! I had forgotten about it. Why hadn't I got rid of the fucking thing! A cold sliver of fear slices my heart.

I begin to cry, silently at first and then with more vigour as I succeed in working myself up. All the time I am wondering what the right reply might be. I can handle this, I know I can. This policewoman will not get the better of me. There is, after all, no need for anyone to know when the water bottle found its way to Cassie's bedside table.

Before I can speak, however, Coombs continues, 'Do you think perhaps that your husband was woken by Cassie during the night and he left it there for her? Was that something he was in the habit of doing?'

Is this where their thinking is bringing them as well – to Daniel? Do they really believe that men are more likely to murder their children than women? How absurd! After all, what do the men care about domestic life! They are never there. They are too busy conquering the world to have any idea what really goes on between a mother and her children. They are not confronted every day with the dreadful tedium of child-minding. They do not comprehend that personality conflicts can exist between a mother and a very young child, daily creating deep wounds of aggravation. They do not understand the shifts of power within a home that can be seismic in their implication. The obvious direction of Coombs's questioning is so bizarre that I feel laughter may soon replace my tears.

I manage not to laugh, however, and the part of my brain that cares desperately about survival files away the useful piece of information this woman has presented to me. The police are looking for something – and someone – to blame. How easy it would be for me to give it to them. How vulnerable Daniel is in the face of their prejudice. I will remember this. There may be a time when the natural instincts of people such as these will come in handy, very handy.

My thoughts are broken as Daniel and Zach re-enter the room. I manage a smile in their direction and then, wiping my eyes with a tissue, I answer Coombs's question.

'I'm sorry, Constable, it's just that I brought her the water bottle and it was the last time I saw her. When I put her to bed, she asked for water and I brought it to her. It wasn't unusual.' Again I sob wholeheartedly.

Daniel sits on the couch beside me and rubs my back. There is silence as Coombs scribbles in her notebook. Obviously she has no more questions. I just wish that she and her colleague would get the hell out of my house.

'If that is all...?' Daniel has read my thoughts.

'It is, sir,' replies Senior Constable Coombs as she closes her notebook. 'Again, please accept our condolences at this very sad time.'

Coombs and Stanley exit and Daniel, Zach and I are left alone in a Cassie-less house. It is a situation which I have fantasised about for months.

TWELVE

I have learned that, with grief, life is lived in lumps of time. There's not much yesterday and very little tomorrow; there is only a pain-filled *now*. Anything else is too much to cope with.

In the *now* that is our first evening without Cassie, Daniel is dealing with his grief through activity. When I enter Zach's room to collect a clean nappy, I find Daniel dismantling Zach's cot. Tears are dripping off his nose. I wonder how he can see properly.

'What are you up to?' I ask.

'This won't fit through the door unless I take it apart.'

'Yes, but why do you want it to fit through the door?'

'Zach's coming in with us. He'll sleep in our room from now on. I want to be able to keep an eye on him. A better eye than I kept on Cassie.'

In with us! We have a three-bedroom home inhabited by three people and we are all supposed to squeeze into one room? Life without Cassie was meant to be easier. I was supposed to be able to sleep. What the hell does Daniel think he is doing?

'I want to be able to monitor his breathing.' He looks at me. 'I was sure you wouldn't mind. I want to be near him. You don't mind, do you?'

Of course I fucking mind, is what I want to scream. 'Of course not,' is what I say.

That first night without Cassie is strangely lonely. Zach, exhausted by the day, falls asleep early. Daniel and I sit on the couch. Sometimes I hear a noise and go to get up, as if I am being called to attend to Cassie. I realise that it will take some time to become accustomed to the fact that I will never have to respond to her demands again. Despite the fear of the impending autopsy, my soul is light; a heavy burden has been forever removed.

We have the receiver of the baby monitor on a table near the couch. It is turned up to its highest setting. The transmitter is near Zach and we can hear his baby breaths as if through a megaphone. At times there are gaps in his breathing and both Daniel and I stare at the monitor, willing the amplified inhalation to begin again. As it does, each time.

I look at the curtains that cover the floor-to-ceiling windows in the dining room. Cassie used to hide behind them. Giggling, she would clutch the edges with her grubby fingers and wait for me to find her. I imagine that I can make out her form behind the greeny blue material. I half expect her to step from behind the curtains and begin to run, looking back at me and laughing and inviting me to follow her. I will miss her games, I think; perhaps I will even miss the strength of her personality. But it is too late for such nostalgia, I tell myself, far too late.

Will her spirit return to haunt me, I wonder. It is easy to believe that her body has been vanquished, but her spirit was so strong.

Daniel speaks. 'She had so much to offer, so fucking much. Even at her age everybody could see that. It seems incredible that someone with as much life as Cassie had, could just go, like that.' He clicks his fingers. 'It can't be as easy as simply turning out a light. It can't be. It can't be that one minute she's here and another minute she isn't. I can't believe that it would fucking end like this. I thought that one day she would be holding my hand as I lay dying. Never, *never* did I think that we would see her go like this.'

'Oh God, Daniel. I agree.' I focus on how cold Cassie felt when we found her and I am able to cry. 'I can imagine her there at the hospital, cold. I was always so careful to make sure that she was never cold. I want to have her here again, so I can keep her warm.'

I rest my head against his shoulder and for a time we are lost in our thoughts. After a while I speak.

'I'll make us both a hot drink.'

I am in the kitchen for some time. When I come out with two cups of steaming tea, Daniel is sitting on the floor with his back against the dining-room wall. He is crying and in his hand he is holding a small plastic hammer. It was one of Cassie's favourite toys. Daniel must have found it behind the curtain.

He has his head resting on his free hand and his shoulders are shaking with his weeping.

A spasm of pain rockets through me. I hate that I have hurt this man. After all, he is the one who replaced my father; the one in whose eyes I am truly special. I remember the Möbius strip. I look to the box on the mantlepiece where it has been kept ever since we moved into this house. I remember how I felt when Daniel gave me that special gift. For the first time ever I felt as if I belonged to someone, as if someone cared about me and me alone.

I feel what I think may be real guilt. Did I do the right thing in the ill-prepared, little more than instinctive action that I performed last night? Was I right to assume the role of the earth goddess in deciding whether or not someone – my daughter, his daughter – would live or die? For in the process I have exposed Daniel to a lifetime of sorrow. It is the same sorrow that I felt when my father died and I know well its full incarnations. I know its sharp edges and blunt jabs, I know its ability to thrust and parry just when one has the gall to believe that the joust has been won. Mastering grief is an unpleasant game in a world that is already too cruel.

But then, what I have done is not so unusual, I tell myself. For centuries unwanted children have been killed, exposed on hillsides, sacrificed to gods and bricked into the foundations of bridges, forts and castles to guarantee the strength of the edifices. Children have been beaten, made to work in mines, bent over looms and bowed under with hard labour. What I have done is simply to build on an ancient tradition where children had no rights and adults determined whether they would be allowed to live or to die.

These days, it is different. Now, such actions are not publicly condoned; as a result of Cassie's death our lives will be rummaged through and dissected. Secrets will be difficult to keep, motivations will not be understood. If the truth is ever revealed what everybody will fail to understand is that what I have done will be for the best. Daniel himself cannot see it yet, but soon things will be more like they were before. He and I will be able to spend more time together. Zach is an easier baby than Cassie. I will organise a regular babysitter. Daniel and I will be able to go out to dinner, to the movies. Things will be as they were in the past. We will be a couple again, instead of simply a mother and father who share the same sleeping space.

I carry the cups of tea over to where Daniel is sitting and place them against the wall. I bend down and take him in my arms. We rock together a little, just the two of us, locked in a grief-laden embrace.

Later that night I conduct a careful search of the house. I collect every one of Cassie's toys and put them in her room. I close the door. I do not want the entire house littered with physical signs of her presence. I don't want Daniel to be hurt again the way he was tonight. I will protect him as much as I am able. After all, I tell myself, it was for him that I did what I did. I have been strong up until now, and I will continue to be strong, until the results of the autopsy are known, until I know whether or not I am really free.

THIRTEEN

The day after Cassie's death, the visitors descend.

They are my third trial, these visitors, and yet another for which I am woefully unprepared. I have had to deal with the doctors, the police, and now comes perhaps my greatest challenge: maintaining my role as grieving mother in front of others, those who expect nothing less than a display of deepest anguish.

The visitors are like vultures, they pick over my shredded emotions, digging deep with their pointed beaks. They bring offerings in exchange for their feasting, of course. There are the obvious gifts: flowers and food, sometimes full meals. But they also bring their own stories of sorrow. Now I am a magnet for other people's tragedies. I'm not sure who are worse: the people who think that their stories give them the insight to know what I am experiencing or those who are desperate to outdo me with the scale of their misfortune. Until now I had not realised what a pathetically tragic world it is. How do people bear the weight of all this personal sorrow?

In the constant presence of these visitors, the necessity for me to play a role is greater than it has ever been, and I wonder that nobody can see me for what I really am. So intense are the projections of what I have done, I feel as if I have the words 'Child Murderer' stamped on my forehead. I am in a state of ceaseless anxiety about the results of the autopsy, but I am obviously unable to share this with anyone. Instead I am forced to talk about my grief, about how much I miss Cassie, about how precious she was. Because what I am feeling is not grief, but fear, my reactions – to my own eyes at least – frequently seem inappropriate. I am not sure when to cry, when to stay silent, how to hold myself, how to deal with Zach in front of other people. The skills of social interaction and appropriate emotional reaction, which I have had to learn over time – those skills which are obviously second nature to other people – desert me. I am in a situation without precedent in my life, and I am adrift in a sea of other people's emotion.

The worst of the visitors are Daniel's parents. They have driven for eight hours, without a break, in their desire to be near us. While they have the good sense not to stay with us, they visit every day, with their endless tears and their memories. We spend one afternoon going through the baby photos, cooing over how beautiful Cassie was. It is so fucking morbid.

Daniel's mother is a big woman, tall and strong and well covered in flesh. She has five children, all of them still alive. She is used to nurturing, used to providing comfort. She closes her arms around me and I feel subsumed by a maternal power I have never before allowed myself to experience.

'You poor dear,' she moans. 'You poor, poor dear. What a dreadful thing to happen to you. You poor dear.'

For a moment I feel as if I may sink into her grief. It is difficult to fight myself free, but when I do, I want nothing more than to scream at her.

Leave me alone, is what I want to cry out. *Just leave me alone, go home to your perfect family and your balanced life and stop feeding off my family and my emotions.*

Above all, I want to be able to live these days in private, to close the door on all my visitors, to be able to do nothing but crawl into a big bed and sleep until I find out the results of the autopsy. I don't want to be an emotional window display for people and their needs.

On the afternoon of the third day Daniel and his father take a walk. I am left alone in the house with his mother. For the first time I become aware of her scrutiny. Her gaze contains the expected sympathy, but in the unusual silence of the house I have the opportunity to see that there is something more to it. Suspicion perhaps? Is it possible, could this woman, this simple, naïve woman, be suspicious of me?

She has never taken to me, I know. I have never been good enough for her youngest son. Daniel was her baby and I took him from her. He is no longer hers; now he is *my* lover, *my* husband.

I tried with this woman when Daniel and I first met. We used to go shopping together sometimes. I would pick out dresses that suited her, that would have looked better on her than the shapeless bags she prefers. A few times she bought the clothes I suggested, but I never saw her wear them. After a while I gave up.

Daniel and I moved soon after we married, back to my home city. I was relieved; Daniel wanted to spend far too much time with his parents for my liking. Now we only have to put up with them a couple of times a year. Probably Daniel's mother has never really liked me. But she has never looked at me quite this way before.

That afternoon I conduct experiments. I carry Zach to the bedroom to change him; she follows. I prepare some baby food – Zach has recently started solids – she watches my every move. I allow her to bathe him and I see her minutely checking his little body. Does she think I am that stupid, I wonder. Still, I cannot help but feel afraid.

That same afternoon Maureen visits. Somehow she has heard about Cassie's death and, despite the false phone number, has managed to track me down.

As soon as I have shown Maureen through to the lounge-room she puts her arms around my back and pulls me to her. She is a squid whose sucker-encrusted tentacles make escape impossible. I am captured, prey to the black ink of her emotion.

'I'm so sorry, so very sorry,' she slobbers. Fat tears roll down her cheeks. Her mascara has smudged.

I shake my head; there is nothing I can say to this woman. Maureen's grief is surreal in its intensity and its focus; after all, I am the one who has lost a child. I feel disgusted by Maureen's overt display of raw emotion, and I want nothing more than to push this woman away from me. I have experienced too many self-centred exhibitions such as this. I have fucking had enough.

'I lost a baby, you know,' Maureen manages through her tears. 'It was when I was pregnant.

I was only two and a half months, but I can understand what you are going through.'

My body grows rigid in anger at Maureen's confession and I breathe deeply in an attempt to control myself. How can the loss of her unformed foetus be likened to my loss? Compared to me she has no idea what tragedy is; she is a charlatan, an impostor.

'Cassie looked like such a beautiful girl,' says Maureen. 'An adorable child.'

My anger with Maureen, with everyone, pushes me off-guard and for a terrible moment I come close to revealing myself.

'Really!' I say. 'In that case it's obvious that you didn't know her.' All my frustration at what Cassie had already succeeded in taking away from me, all the pent-up anxiety over what the autopsy will reveal, all my anger at the visitors who will not leave us alone, and the fear I have over the suspicions of Daniel's mother come out in that sentence. I am careless.

Maureen looks at me. I see her fat white forehead wrinkle as she tries to work out what I mean.

I am horrified at my indiscretion, and I search desperately for an escape from my loose words.

'What I mean,' I say, 'is that since it's obvious you didn't know her, I appreciate it all the more that you've made the effort to visit today.'

Is it enough? Maureen's brow unfurrows a little, but I am unsure if she has accepted the renegotiation of my original meaning.

I wait, and between the two of us there is an awkward silence. I, who have been so careful to act appropriately over the past few days, may have made a trap for myself. *Not now*, I want to scream, *not now, not here, not in front of this woman.*

Suddenly, I hear footsteps. Daniel and his father have returned from their walk and Daniel has come to see who I am talking to.

I carry out the necessary introductions.

'Daniel, this is Maureen, we used to go to school together. Maureen, Daniel, my husband.'

Daniel and Maureen shake hands. Her podgy one inside his.

'Yes, I remember.' Daniel is nodding, his smile warm and sincere. 'That day in the park; we didn't have the chance to be introduced. It's lovely to meet you.'

'And you.' Maureen is nodding and smiling also. Smiling does not suit her; it emphasises the awful lines at the corners of her eyes. 'But I'm sorry, the circumstances are so sad. I can remember Cassie that day in the park. I remember her running. She was so alive. What an awful thing to happen to her, to you all.'

'Yes,' says Daniel – he is struggling to keep his composure – 'I wouldn't wish this grief on anyone, but it's good that you've come. We've been overwhelmed by the visitors we've had. Even people who didn't know Cassie have come.'

'Like me,' says Maureen. 'I've already been thanked for that.'

She has chosen to let my comment pass! I gulp, a turtle coming up for air. I had not realised that I'd been holding my breath.

As I escape the room on the pretext of making some tea I can hear Daniel repeating to Maureen, 'It's so good that you've come.'

I am shaking at the thought of what I have almost revealed.

FOURTEEN

That night I sleep badly. I swim in the world of the dead. It is a world where my daughter reaches out to me endlessly in a silent scream, where floating, faceless eyes watch my every move, my every reaction, where strong arms hold me hard. In my dream I am fighting for my freedom, for my life, for my right to be what I need to be. In my dream fingers proclaiming guilt point at me.

Afterwards, I cannot sleep because I cannot allow those images to claim me.

I rise and slip into my dressing-gown. I make myself a cup of tea. There are too many hours between now and dawn. Too many hours for me to fill, and I cannot – will not – return to my tortured sleep.

Holding my cup, I wander from room to room. The dining room is unswept and empty, the lounge cold and dark with its curtains drawn. I walk down the hall to Zach's room. A mobile still hangs from the ceiling. Decorations remain on the walls, but the room looks purposeless with the cot and occupant removed.

I move further down the corridor. I cannot help myself. The door to Cassie's room is closed. It has remained closed over the last few days. Daniel will allow no one in there. One day he will have to confront its emptiness, but not yet.

I open the door; the hinges squeak. I had been meaning to oil them before Cassie died. My heart pounds. I am almost afraid to enter this room that has become a shrine to our daughter. A sliver of moonlight through the curtains shows me the way across the room to the night-light. I flick it on. Its shade is decorated with fairies and it casts a pink glow over the room. I lean over Cassie's cot, its quilt covered in fairy fabric. I trace my finger over a fairy wing. We had given Cassie pink fairy wings for her first birthday. They were covered in glitter. She had worn them the day before she died. I am still sweeping glitter from the kitchen floor.

I did love my daughter, I think defiantly, *I did love her.* But of course I had not loved her enough. I had not loved her enough to allow her to take everything that was mine, and I certainly had not loved her enough to allow her death to ruin me. And now I am afraid. I am afraid that what I have done may not be sufficient to earn me the freedom I need.

I think about Doctor Hadid and Senior Constable Coombs. I think about their suspicions and prejudices. I think about things that might have happened. I think about alternatives and possibilities.

If I close my eyes I can hear Cassie calling out the night she died. I can hear both Daniel and myself turning over in our sleep, neither of us wanting to be the one who will have to respond to her. But then I can feel the mattress lift a little as Daniel swings his legs to the floor and rises from the bed. I hear the light switch being turned on in the kitchen. I hear the sound of Daniel removing a water bottle from the cupboard, the sound of it being filled with water and the top being screwed on; I hear the sound of the kitchen light being turned off, and perhaps, if I listen carefully enough, I can hear Daniel's footsteps on the carpet as he tiptoes past our room, past Zach's room and down to Cassie's. I can hear the small squeak as her door is pushed open, and the sound of Cassie grumbling as she reaches for the bottle and lifts it to her mouth. And then, if I were to be honest, I would have to admit that perhaps I dozed and heard nothing more... well, nothing more until the small squeak as Cassie's door was swung closed and my husband returned to the bed, now cold on his side.

These are the things I might be able to remember if I am pushed, if I am threatened. And if pushed more I might remember the strain Daniel had been under at work and how it impacted on his patience and ability to deal with the children; how he had been complaining that the children were still waking us at night. I might be able to recall some incidents when he had been unreasonably angry, with us all, but with Cassie in particular. I might remember all these things and many more. It's amazing what one is capable of remembering when placed under sufficient pressure.

I think that I will write down what I have remembered. It is important that things are written down. People believe what they see on paper. I will feel better after I have done that, safer. I will be able to return to bed; I may even be able to sleep.

FIFTEEN

On the morning of the fifth day the phone rings. Daniel answers it. I hover in the background, trying to work out to whom he is speaking. It is Doctor Hadid. My heart hammers. I strain to overhear what Daniel is saying, but the conversation is over almost as soon as it has begun.

I am standing virtually on top of Daniel as he puts down the receiver.

'What did he want?' My desperate excitement has made me breathless. 'What did he say? What news does he have?'

Daniel puts out his hand and grabs my arm as if to steady me, or maybe it is himself he is concerned about.

'They have the report.'

'The autopsy report! What does it say? Have they found out what happened?'

'Doctor Hadid hasn't told me yet. We both agreed that it was better for him to explain things face to face. I made a time for us to go down to the hospital this afternoon.'

This afternoon! I have waited four days to discover what my future will be. I don't know if I can wait any longer. I feel as if I might scream.

'He says it should only take half an hour or so.'

That little, I think.

'Did he give you any idea?' I ask.

Daniel shakes his head. 'No, and I didn't ask. I thought it would be easier if we were there together. Maybe he can explain things to us that we would have trouble understanding otherwise.'

Yes, that is true, I think, especially if they have found out what really killed Cassie. There are not many people who could understand it, who could understand the forces that drove me to kill my daughter. Even if people had been privy to my deepest, driving emotions they would have trouble understanding it.

Perhaps there are some things which are not meant to be understood, merely accepted.

By the time we arrive at the front desk of the hospital my nerves are stretched tight. There is a slight humming in my ears, the sound of a distant jet engine or a persistent fly. I am a tuning fork resonating at an extreme pitch.

Doctor Hadid is here to greet us. He is still in his white coat. This time, however, we are shown into his office. It is extremely small and messy. Piles of papers ring the floor. The shelves are full of books; some lie horizontally over others. I balance Zach on my lap. There is no space for him anywhere else. The room smells of old dust and half-drunk coffee. It is so stuffy I can barely breathe.

The doctor, the good doctor on whom my future rests, picks up a folder and clears his throat. 'Well, as you know, I received the autopsy report this morning and I considered it best for us to talk through it together.'

I am squeezing Zach's arms so tightly that he squirms in protest. *Surely*, I am thinking, *it must be okay, they couldn't have found anything wrong or we wouldn't be sitting here like this.* Or is this a set-up? Will armed police leap from behind the filing cabinets as soon as Doctor Hadid has revealed the findings of the report? I am not sane at the moment.

'Please,' says Daniel, 'we are both anxious to know what the report has found. We are both desperate to know what happened to Cassie.'

I nod; incapable of speech.

'Well,' says Doctor Hadid, 'I'm afraid that the findings will come as somewhat of a disappointment in that regard. The official cause of death has been given as undetermined.'

'Undetermined,' Daniel and I sing in unison. I am genuinely surprised. I had hoped Cassie's death would be put down to SIDS; I had not expected to encounter this nebulous 'undetermined' finding. I am suspicious it could morph into something sinister, something that might turn around and bite me. I am not sure whether I can relax yet.

Doctor Hadid nods. 'Yes, I am afraid that on the face of it a finding like this doesn't seem to tell us a lot, but from a medical point of view it *is* quite informative. It tells us that Cassie didn't die from an unexpected asthma attack; that she didn't die as a result of a severe allergic reaction to something; that she wasn't poisoned, or interfered with in any way...as far as we can tell. A finding of death from undetermined causes eliminates most things, but unfortunately for me as a doctor and for you, as Cassie's parents, it doesn't tell us what *did* cause her death.'

Daniel nods, 'That's right, it doesn't.'

I manage to speak. 'But what about SIDS? I thought that if a young child like Cassie died unexpectedly then it was usually due to SIDS.'

'Well,' says Doctor Hadid. 'The generally recognised definition of SIDS is of a sudden, unexplained death occurring in an infant under the age of twelve months. That doesn't mean, of course, that children of Cassie's age don't die suddenly and inexplicably. It's just that their deaths are not normally recorded as SIDS, but rather as death due to undetermined or unexplained causes.' Doctor Hadid spreads his hands in a gesture of futility. 'Not that the distinction is important for you, of course. Unfortunately the finding simply means what it says; we just don't know what Cassie died from.'

Daniel leans forward, his elbows on Doctor Hadid's desk. 'So, Doctor, does that mean that we have to be extra careful with Zach? Is it possible that he could be more susceptible to something like this happening?'

'Actually no,' replies Doctor Hadid. 'Most large studies on infants and children who have died suddenly and inexplicably, indicate no increase of unexplained death in subsequent siblings. In fact, the prevailing wisdom now is that if more than one child in a family dies from what appears to be unde-termined causes, then the real cause of death is more likely to be something else.'

'Such as?' asks Daniel.

'Such as homicide, usually by one of the parents.'

I feel Daniel shudder beside me. I begin to sob. Is this a warning? I think not, but there is not very much about which I can be sure right now.

Doctor Hadid's warm, brown eyes meet mine. 'I understand that the very notion is abhorrent to most people, but such events do occur and, unfor-tunately, unless there are obvious signs of trauma, they can be very difficult to pick up in young children.' He turns his attention back to Daniel. 'So, to answer your question, sir, I can say with near certainty that your son will not die from sudden, unexplained causes. Zach is as likely as any of us to live to one hundred and one.'

There is silence as Daniel and I allow that to sink in.

Finally, Daniel speaks. 'Well, I'm pleased that we don't need to have any particular worry for Zach. We've both been very concerned about him. But, Doctor, what I wanted, what we both need, I think, is some explanation for Cassie's death. Death from undetermined causes tells us nothing. We're left with no answers, no reason, no way in which we can understand this dreadful tragedy.'

Doctor Hadid nods and clears his throat again. He looks uncomfortable. 'I understand. I really wish I could tell you more. I am never happy with a finding such as this. For me, it asks more questions than it answers.' He looks at each of us in turn. His eyes are gentle, but probing. They are eyes which are not satisfied by unanswered questions. 'Unfortunately, however,' Doctor Hadid continues, 'the finding means what it says. We have no way of telling what Cassie died from. Sometimes things like this happen, even to the healthiest of infants and children. It is inexplicable, it is terrible, but I'm afraid that I can tell you no more.'

I begin to cry again. I have been doing it a lot lately. I am becoming really rather good at it, but this time neither of the two men in the room could guess the real cause of my tears. I am crying with relief.

Doctor Hadid picks up a piece of paper from his desk.

'Here are the contact details of the local parents' bereavement support group. The hospital also has a counsellor on staff; I have written her name and contact details on the bottom of the paper. Please remember, these people are here for you. Sometimes the strain of a loss such as this can manifest itself in unexpected ways. I urge you not to feel that you must deal with things alone.'

It is Daniel's and my turn to nod. We agree that we will probably take up the offer of the counsellor. With that, our interview is at an end and we are free to leave this stifling room, free to face the sun, free to farewell our daughter and to continue with the rest of our lives. I'm not stupid; I realise, of course, that Doctor Hadid may be suspicious, but I have outplayed better people than him in my life. He may have his suspicions, but I am free, free and Cassie-less. I am giddy with the wonder of it all.

SIXTEEN

We decide to cremate our precious child. Neither Daniel nor I can bear the thought of her in the cold dark ground. Cassie will remain in an urn on a special shelf in the living room. She will never be cold. She will always be with us, where I can see her, where she will be within my ultimate control.

The ceremony is held on a bright early spring day; the world has taken on crystal hues. The unusual light makes everything seem brittle, hard but somehow unstable. The trees on the hill overlooking the crematorium appear to be etched against the sky. There is a very slight breeze blowing. A lightness fills my body and soul. I am so ridiculously free and unencumbered that I feel I may float into the sparse air.

As we approach the stone chapel, the gravel pathway crunches beneath our feet. I recall a medieval carving I once saw where crusaders marched their way over the bones of hundreds of children. There are many sacrifices that have to be made in the fight for true freedom, the carving was saying. My personal experience has now told me how true that is.

I clutch Daniel's arm with my left hand and hold Zach with my right. Daniel and I are dressed in black. Zach is in dark blue. We look appropriately dignified, a family in deep mourning. As, of course, we are. Except for Zach who still finds the world a joke, sister or no sister. He has handfuls of my hair and is pulling with all the power of his six-kilogram body.

My dress is new, bought especially for the occasion. It is fitted and extremely flattering. My skin is pale from winter and the stress of the past week. I have added chestnut highlights to my hair. It glows in the mid-morning sunlight. I know how good I look.

It seems as if hundreds of people have chosen to attend the service. I make eye contact with a few of them; I nod and smile and murmur thank yous to those who have come out today to witness our deepest sorrow. I am determined to play well the tragic figure, the strong but suffering mother. After all, I know the importance of rituals such as this in shaping people's perceptions.

We enter the chapel and make our way to the front row of seats, just behind the coffin. Daniel chose it. It is very small, and pink. Cassie would have approved. I chose the dress she is wearing. It is green, her best one. It has been worn only once before. I remember the occasion well. It was the birthday party of a little friend. Cassie had danced in the dress, its full skirt flaring out as she had spun around. Daniel said that she looked like a fairy princess. He loved her in that dress. He cried when I told him it was the one I picked for her to wear today.

Once Daniel, Zach and I have settled ourselves in the chapel others follow. Sounds and smells wash into the enclosed space. There is coughing and clearing of throats, an occasional blown nose. I hear someone whisper my name. Perfumes and aftershaves clash in their fight for dominance. In my imagination the individual mourners meld together, as if a great grey beast with many tentacles lies at my back. Its presence is almost overpowering.

A thickset man stands up and approaches the microphone. He is the chaplain we have chosen. He has an extremely melodious voice. He talks about Cassie as if he knew her. But, of course, he didn't. He didn't know her will; he didn't know her determination; he didn't know what she was capable of.

When it is time I hand Zach to Daniel and make my way to the microphone. Now the quiet rustling, which had accompanied even the chaplain's words, is subdued. People lean forward to better hear what I have to say. I know they must be intrigued. It is unusual for a mother to speak at the funeral of her infant daughter. There is awe that I am standing here, and wonder at what I will say. I had forgotten how satisfying it is to have an audience, a collection of people hanging off my every word. I will enjoy this. I clear my throat.

'Cassie was with us for such a painfully short time, but it was a time which changed the lives of our family and indeed the lives of all who had the privilege of knowing her. Cassie impressed everyone with her vigour and spirit: she was a flame in a room of darkness; a breath of fresh air on a still day; a ray of sunshine breaking the gloom. Her body and her awesome will might no longer be with us, but her memory and the joy which she brought to us all during her short life always will be.'

Daniel's mother, that most annoying of women, sobs so violently that she drowns out my words. I lean closer to the microphone, raise my voice and continue. 'I have a poem which I would like to share with you. It's called "The Water-Lily" and it was written by Henry Lawson in 1890.

'A lonely young wife
In her dreaming discerns
A lily-decked pool
With a border of ferns,
And a beautiful child,
With butterfly wings,
Trips down to the edge of the water and sings:
"Come, mamma! come!
Quick! follow me–
Step out on the leaves of the water-lily!"

And the lonely young wife,
Her heart beating wild,

Cries, "Wait till I come,
Till I reach you, my child!"
But the beautiful child
With butterfly wings
Steps out on the leaves of the lily and sings:
"Come, mamma! come!
Quick! follow me!
And step on the leaves of the water-lily!"

And the wife in her dreaming
Steps out on the stream,
But the lily leaves sink
And she wakes from her dream.
Ah, the waking is sad,
For the tears that it brings,
And she knows 'tis her dead baby's spirit that sings:
"Come, mamma! come!
Quick! follow me!
Step out on the leaves of the water-lily!"'

By the time I have finished the poem the chapel is filled with the sound of weeping. I have not lost the ability to influence people with my oratory. A cold surge of power tears through me. I am overcome with emotion. I press my handkerchief to my eyes.

It is all I can do to make my way back to my seat and reclaim Zach.

Now it is Daniel's turn to take the floor. He speaks of his joy in having known Cassie and how he refuses to mourn too much because, no matter how short a time she was with us, it was a privilege to have been her parents. I sob uncontrollably. Someone puts an arm around me and someone else takes Zach away.

I am not the only one crying. People cry for us, they cry for Cassie, but generally they cry for themselves. I know this most of all: people are fundamentally selfish. It is not only for the soul of Cassie that people cry. It is for the soul of others who have died and others who may die. There are many present who will hug their loved ones a bit harder this evening. The grief of our family has simply been a catalyst for theirs.

The service has ended and once more we step into the brittle outside world. Streams of people come up to offer me their condolences; the whispered messages are endless, repetitive, unimaginative. Someone has taken Zach from me again and I have no shield against the barrage of sorrow everyone directs towards me. I shake hands, kiss cheeks, blink back tears. It is all terribly difficult. Daniel and I are separated for a time and I panic. We have shared our sorrow for the past week. I don't know if I can do it without him. I feel as if my grief-mask may crack.

A bit longer, I tell myself, *just a bit longer; you are nearly there. The river has almost been forded; you are nearly at the other side.*

With relief I see a blond head above the crowd. It is Daniel. As I am pushing people out of the way to reach him, someone calls my name and I hesitate for a second. It is Maureen. Hasn't she intruded on our grief enough? At least this time I am prepared for her. As she lurches towards me I step back so that she is unable to hug me.

Maureen trawls through her handbag until she finds a tissue. 'That was a beautiful ceremony,' she sniffles. 'And your speech, I don't know how you had the strength to do it.'

'Thank you,' I say, 'it wasn't easy.' I wave madly at Daniel. Thankfully he sees me and makes his way over.

'Maureen,' he says, 'it's so nice to see you again. I'm so glad you could come today. It's wonderful to have your support.'

'Yes, isn't it,' I nod. My tone is dismissive and at the same time I begin to move away from Maureen, towards the car. I expect Daniel to follow, but, I see to my horror that his eyes have filled with tears, his shoulders have collapsed forward as if he must protect his heart. He has not cried all day and I am not prepared for his tears now. I pause for a moment and a moment is all it takes for Maureen to step into my gap. She has her tissue, which she is pressing into his hand, she has one arm around him pulling him to her, she has her head on his shoulder next to his head, she is whispering something to him. I cannot hear, I cannot hear what she is saying. Her mouth is so close to his ear that I think perhaps he would be able to feel the small drops of water vapour that are expelled as she speaks. Daniel leans into her. I imagine her soft, large breasts pressed against his chest. I imagine their hearts beating in unison, left heart to right breast, right breast to left heart. I am appalled at the liberties she is taking; I am aghast that Daniel is allowing himself to become so close to another woman in my presence. I am standing by myself in the crowd of people drifting around me. Only Maureen and Daniel are anchored, only Maureen and Daniel are comforted. I am alone.

I am so dreadfully alone. They are making a spectacle of themselves; they are making a spectacle of me!

I picture myself stepping between them, pushing them apart. It would be like opening the jaws of an oyster shell. I would expose its grey glutinous heart. I would spear it with a stick. I would expose it to the sun, to wither and die slowly. I would take pleasure in my actions.

And then they, Maureen and Daniel, step apart. Together they look at me and I wonder what it is that they see. I wonder.

The crowd has thinned enough for us to make our way to the car. There will be some family at a small wake, but not too many people. I reclaim Zach and he seems to wink at me. It is a long slow wink that obscures one grey eye – an eye that is not at all like mine.

SEVENTEEN

My mother has decided to grace Cassie's wake with her presence. She has turned up for the occasions in my life she has deemed suitably important – my birth, the death of my father, my marriage, the days after the birth of my children. At other times she has been mercifully absent: sometimes metaphorically, sometimes literally.

My mother insisted on organising the catering for the wake and so we have food that is completely unsuited to mourning. There is too much finger food, light and tangy with no depth of taste or sustenance. I had never considered it before, but as I bite into a caviar-laden rice biscuit, I realise that some foods are appropriate to grief: warm potato chips, chicken soup which has simmered for hours, bread heavily smeared with butter. But my mother wouldn't understand the importance of that kind of food; she has been starving herself for the whole of her adult life.

Zach is with my mother now. She is whispering into his ear. Her hair is ridiculously spiky and red, her skirt too short, her skinny knees too knobbly. She resembles an expensively dressed street urchin – one of her guises; it has fooled many intelligent people before now. Zach is cooing at her. The secret is obviously a good one. I will never be privy to it, of course. My mother has never included me among her initiates.

Daniel moves over to them and tickles Zach's feet. He has been doing the rounds. 'Thank you for coming,' he has murmured over and over again. I can see that fatigue and grief have reduced him to a robot. 'Thank you for coming, thank you for coming, thank you for coming.' I can imagine him doing it in a Dalek-type voice. Now Zach giggles in delight at Daniel's attention and my mother joins in. Her ridiculously white false teeth flash at Daniel. I am almost nauseated to see that he smiles back.

I have been drinking all afternoon; Mother has provided sherry for our guests. At least she had the sense to refrain from the champagne that she normally prefers. I will ask Daniel to give Zach a bottle tonight instead of me feeding him. I don't want to give the boy alcohol poisoning. Suddenly the idea of that seems horribly funny. I realise that I am drunk.

One of my long-lost cousins appears in front of me, blocking my view of the happy threesome.

'How're you going?' He speaks with a slight drawl. I think he is a carpenter.

'I'm okay,' I reply. I have plumbed the depths of grief far too often today to offer him anything more than this.

'She's a funny old bird.'

'Who?' I genuinely have no idea whom he is talking about.

'Your mum.'

'Oh yes, her.'

'Haven't seen her in a while.'

Lucky you, I think. Aloud I say, 'Me neither.'

'She still looks good.'

'Yes.' *If you like chicken legs.*

'Remember how she chased us when we were kids, that time we pinched her undies off the line? Rob put them on, remember; they were purple.'

'Lilac,' I correct him. I do remember the time. My mother was terribly embarrassed, as she should have been. The pants were brief and the bra padded. I thought them completely unsuitable for a woman her age, although at the time she was not much older than I am now.

My cousin looks over at my mother. 'I think I had a thing for her when I was young. She was kind of exotic, you know.'

I nearly choke. The masturbatory longing of my cousin for my mother is not something I feel like discussing now.

My cousin examines me searchingly. He was the first person with whom I shared a cigarette. He knows me pretty well, even though we haven't seen each other for a while. After all, it is only at times like this that I allow my family to force themselves upon me.

'You look like her,' he says.

I purse my lips as if I have tasted acid.

'You've never liked her, have you?' he continues.

I don't bother to respond to this statement of genius. She, my mother, is looking over at us. I raise my glass in a half salute. The last thing I want to do is encourage her to come over.

My cousin is still talking. 'She's not so bad, you know. She helped me a lot with my schoolwork after Mum died and she did a lot of cooking for us. Do you remember?'

No, I certainly don't remember that. I remember my cousin living next door and I remember his mother, my aunt, my mother's sister, dying. She was knocked down by a bus and died in hospital a few days later. My cousin was almost fifteen. I was thirteen. All I can remember from that year is my mother being terribly absent, absent at a time when I needed her, at a time when we might have been able to forge the friendship, the mutual regard, which has always eluded us. I have never forgiven her for that.

And now I am talking with my mother. She has one hand above my elbow and she is squeezing. She surveys the room. It is almost empty. Despite the lack of comfort in her food, most of it has been consumed. She is pleased by this. She has provided; I am in her debt.

'I don't usually go to funerals,' she confides. It is spoken breezily, as if she has just proclaimed that she doesn't 'do lunch', or can't wear yellow.

'No,' I reply. I also cannot imagine her at funerals – not enough colour, too many tears.

'Your father's death ruined them for me.' Another dreadful thing which my father has done to her. My mother blames, has always blamed, my father for as much as she can. She blames him for the estrangement with her family, for her wrinkles, for the fact that she and I do not get on.

But I also have been thinking of my father today. He died when I was eleven, nearly twelve. Our family has been unlucky with accidents. My father had woken in the night and gone into the kitchen to get a glass of water. It was unusual for him to do this; it was usually Mother who had problems sleeping. What was also unusual that night was that, somehow, a bottle of oil had leaked over the floor. He slipped and hit his head against my mother's prized granite benchtop. My mother found him the next morning. Later she told me that it looked as if he had bled oil all over the floor. There was no actual blood –

the wound itself was very small, just enough to have killed him. A freak accident, the police called it.

The day after his funeral my periods began for the first time. I was lying with my feet up on the couch, watching television. My mother entered the room...perhaps 'waltzed' is the correct word. It was the day after my father's funeral and she began to talk to me about clothes, fucking clothes. I could barely see the television, my eyes were so swollen from crying, and she wanted to discuss fashion. She knew we would get some insurance money as a result of my father's death and she was planning how to spend it.

'I can buy a new summer wardrobe. You'll need some new things too, darling. Pink's in this year, I see. You look good in pink; everybody looks good in pink. We can paint the house. Tom and I have been wanting to do that for years. Poor dear Tom! We can only do these things now that he's gone.' From the depths of her bosom she withdrew a handkerchief, part of the previous day's funeral attire. It was black with a dainty lace border, also black – my mother always was the queen of accessorising. She dabbed daintily at her eyes with it.

'Poor Tom. Your poor daddy.'

It was too much for me.

'It's your fault!' I screamed at her. 'You've taken him away from me. You should be happy. *He* shouldn't have died. It's your fault he died.'

My mother looked at me. I couldn't tell what was going on behind those black-rimmed eyes.

'You never loved him properly, and you hated it that we got on so well together.' I was almost sobbing now; my fists were clenched. Never had I hated anyone as much as I hated my mother then.

My mother began to shake slightly. I could see that she was controlling her own temper with difficulty. I didn't care. I was surfing on pure emotion, a bit more only added to the surge.

She exhaled heavily; her breath was sour and old. It clashed with her sweet, awful, chemist-brand perfume. I thought I might throw up.

She leaned over as if to give me a hug, but I pushed her away and swung my legs off the couch so I was sitting upright. I felt as if her perfume would suffocate me.

'Don't touch me you bitch,' I yelled. She recoiled at the use of that word. I had never sworn in front of her before, but I was angry.

'Daddy told me what you said. Two days before he died. He told me that you thought I was spoilt; that you said he was going to ruin me by giving in to me too much. I know that you always hated it that he treated me as if I was special. And now you're happy, happy that he died. YOU BITCH.'

My mother slapped me on the face.

In my imagination the sound of that slap echoed around the room. It has certainly echoed through both our lives.

For a moment neither of us moved. I could feel where each of my mother's fingers had connected with my face. I knew that I would never forgive her. My mother sat firm and rigid as the adrenaline of her anger washed through her. And then, she slumped.

'You're tired,' she said. 'Having your period for the first time is difficult. I'll forget what you just said to me, and I think you should too. I'll tell you what I hope. I hope that you and I can be friends. I hope that if anything positive comes out of your father's death, it is that we become friends.'

As usual my mother was too optimistic. She and I never did become friends.

The night after the fight with my mother, I crept to my father's wardrobe and took out one of his shirts, the one that smelled most strongly of him. That night, and for many after, I slept with it beside me. When it lost the smell of my father I ironed it. The heat brought out the aroma of his sweat and deodorant. I have always been very olfactory.

Cassie's wake is finished. Finally Daniel and I are able to crawl into bed. We are exhausted. He has deep purple circles under his eyes.

'Thank God that's over,' he says.

Perhaps he is thinking what I am. Now we can get on with our lives.

I roll over towards him. As usual he is naked. He is smooth-skinned and slightly downy, like a young deer. I begin to play with his nipples, they harden under my fingers and suddenly I am so hungry for him that my mouth goes dry. I want this man. I want him like I wanted a pink bicycle when I was a child, like I wanted my mother to tell me how much she loved me, like I wanted that blue dress that hung in Casey's window. He is the amalgam of all my yearnings.

I lick his purple eyes. They are salty with dried tears. His lashes gum together with my saliva and I separate them with my fingertips, gentle, oh so gentle. He used to give me butterfly kisses when we first met. He would be so close that I could feel the wet feather of his breath.

Daniel is hard now, but his eyes are still closed. I hold him first with my hands and then with my lips. I feel the hard beneath the soft. It is everything I have always loved about him; he is steel beneath fairy floss, but it was always the strength I needed.

He joins my movements. I know that he needs me more than ever and now his body knows it also. I have always been good at this game, good at opening the trap of flesh that makes men want more and more. For a while it has been forgotten. But I know that I will reclaim the power that is mine.

Later Daniel cries as he lies beside me.

'Poor baby,' I whisper. 'Poor baby.'

EIGHTEEN

*I*n the weeks following the funeral we learn to live without our eldest child. Daniel has started tentatively back at work. Often he lasts for only half a day. When he returns home he slumps in an armchair. He doesn't do anything, just slumps. For long periods of time he barely speaks, or eats, or sleeps. Grief has made him inert. He looks pitiful, as if he has shrunk. His cheeks are sucked in; he is stooped; he shaves badly or not at all.

I caution myself to be patient with this lassitude of Daniel's. I have read about the stages of grief; I know that they take time to live through. But I want so desperately for Daniel to be happy again, as I am. I want so desperately for us to be able to move on with our lives that sometimes I make mistakes; sometimes I stumble; sometimes I reveal the depth of my impatience.

One Friday night I prepare a special dinner. I light candles. I burn aromatic oils. I greet Daniel at the door with a kiss. Tonight I am determined that we will sit across the table from each other and talk about something other than Cassie. Tonight I want to shake Daniel out of his lethargy and guilt. I want him to see things as I do, to recognise that this event, terrible as it may have been, opens up all sorts of possibilities for us. I want to show him that this is not the end, that it is in fact a beginning of sorts, a time to make up for the mistakes of the past eighteen months or so, a time when we can pull together as a couple again. Tonight I am impatient.

Dinner is a success. Daniel appreciates my effort. He comments on each course. It looks as if the night will be everything I hoped.

After a while we move to the couch. I have bought Daniel's favourite dessert wine; we sip it while nibbling on a cheese platter.

I rest one hand on Daniel's thigh.

'I have a surprise,' I announce.

'Another one?' Daniel is almost laughing. I can tell that tonight has done him good. 'What is it?'

'I've hired a babysitter for tomorrow night. I thought that you and I could go out, have dinner or see a movie. We haven't done that in so long. We can have Zach asleep before she comes. He won't even know that we've gone.'

'No!' Daniel's reply is instant.

'No?' I am not sure if I have heard correctly.

'No. I won't leave Zach in the care of anyone outside the family. First of all he's too young, and after what happened to Cassie, I don't trust anyone else to take care of him.'

'But you heard what Doctor Hadid said,' I reply. 'There is virtually no chance that Zach will die unexpectedly. Nothing will happen to him whether we are here with him or not.'

Daniel is shaking his head. 'No, I don't want to do it. I *can't* do it. I think about Cassie all the time. I feel there must have been something we could have done or shouldn't have done that might have saved her.'

For fuck's sake! I feel as if I will scream. *When are you going to fucking move on? When are we going to be able to get on with our fucking lives without sitting around playing funeral dirges and tiptoeing around the shrine of guilt that our daughter's memory has become?*

Outwardly I say, 'I understand, Daniel. But we have to think about moving on, getting on with our lives, filling our lives.'

'Don't you feel that?' Daniel continues. He has not heard anything I have said. He has me captured in the intensity of his gaze, and like a transfixed animal I am forced to reply to his original statement.

I sigh. 'Daniel, I don't know. Maybe. Maybe there was something we could have done. That was what we hoped the autopsy would tell us, I suppose. But we'll never know.'

'I just can't help thinking... If she'd eaten lamb instead of beef that night; if she'd had a different quilt cover; if she'd worn different pyjamas – would any of it have made a difference? If we'd kept the baby monitor in her room; if she'd been sleeping in the same room as Zach – would *that* have made a difference?' His voice is raised. 'If the room was cleaner; if the window was open; if she hadn't had pneumonia a few weeks earlier – would any of these things have made a difference?' He is shouting now. He is angry and grief-stricken and confused all at once. He is shaking his fist at fate, demanding answers from the gods, insisting that he *know*. His profile is upraised, his skin tight, his eyes shine with near madness. He is magnificent.

And then he collapses. His head drops forward; his shoulders slump. He is crying great sobs of anger and denial. I put both my arms around him and hold him close to me. It will not be enough, I know, but it is required that I at least make an attempt to comfort him.

'I just wish I knew,' he keens. I am reminded of women in war-torn countries whom I have heard on the television news crying for their dead sons. Their lament is as old as the world. 'I just wish I knew.'

Suddenly Daniel's head snaps up, looking at me, eyes so close to mine. 'Did you hear anything that night?' he demands. I am unprepared for this near accusation. My head jerks back as if to protect myself from his words but as I see the tears continue to well in his eyes I realise that all he wants is the reassurance that I couldn't have done anything; that neither of us is responsible for Cassie's death.

'Nothing,' I whisper. 'This has tortured me too, Daniel. Don't think I haven't gone through all this. I wonder if she made any noise before she stopped breathing, and perhaps if I'd been able to hear it, I might have been able to change things... But you know what, Daniel? I've come to the conclusion that there is absolutely nothing either of us could have done. Cassie's death was as inevitable as her birth; it was woven into a pattern of fate that nothing and nobody could have prevented.'

Daniel is looking intently at me. For an uneasy moment I wonder if he has seen through my carefully chosen words.

Finally he says, 'You've always been a fatalist, haven't you? I wish I could share your easy acceptance that some things are preordained.'

'Oh Daniel, all I'm trying to say is that you must stop torturing yourself about this. There was *nothing* we could have done to have prevented it.'

Daniel rests his head against my shoulder. I run my fingers through his hair. I am afraid that he will begin to cry, but his breathing remains regular. Maybe, I dare hope, maybe if I can make Daniel see some of the opportunities which Cassie's death has brought, then maybe this will be a turning point in his grieving. Maybe, just maybe, I will be able to reclaim my husband.

'Have you thought,' I begin, 'of what we can do with Cassie's room? I was thinking we could turn it into a study. I've got a nice paint colour picked out...'

I feel Daniel stiffen. He sits upright and for a few moments he stares at me. Then he rises from the couch and puts on his shoes. The door is slammed hard behind him.

NINETEEN

Nearly six weeks after Cassie's funeral I decide the time is right to return to my mothers' group.

The host for the get-together today is May. She is the oldest member of the group. She has one child, a boy, James. He was born after several attempts at IVF, and May dotes on him. He is spoilt rotten and very, very naughty. Despite her son, everyone likes May and everyone enjoys going to her house. She has old-fashioned armchairs and a coffee table made for putting one's feet up on. Her garden is semi-wild and the older toddlers disappear into it, emerging only when it is time to go home. May is the wise woman of the group. If anyone has a problem, she knows about it; if anyone needs help, she offers it. I will feel comfortable at May's.

The get-together goes something like this.

Silence as Zach and I enter the room and then, too quickly, renewed conversation. May comes over and hugs me. I've never been hugged by so many people as I have over the weeks since Cassie's death. I have always protected my personal space; I don't like people to touch me too often or with familiarity. No one rubbed my stomach when I was pregnant. Today, however, leaning awkwardly over Zach, who is on the floor at my feet, I am forced to hug May back. Our cheeks connect. May is wearing sandal-wood perfume. It reminds me of a necklace I bought in Asia. It was carved from sandalwood and for years its fragrance scented my jewellery box.

Thankfully May doesn't say anything. Should I pull away? I never know when to end these things. I think that May is waiting for me to release her and so we hug until Zach screams for my attention.

I pick him up and gradually the other mothers come over to pay their respects at the altar of great sorrow.

'If there's anything I can do.'

'Call any time.'

'I'll be here if you ever need me.'

They are uttering platitudes. We all know it.

Only Rachael does not come over to me. She is sitting on the couch and I try to catch her eye so that she can offer at least a nod in recognition of my situation. But no, she will not give me even that.

After a time I make my way over to her.

'I suppose you heard of my loss?' I say.

Rachael nods, lowers her eyes and sips her tea. 'Yes, it must have been terrible for you.'

How right she is. *Yes, it was terrible for me.* No one else has seemed to understand this. Losing a child is not only sorrowful, it is also difficult and inconvenient. One is on constant public display. One has to be solicitous of other people and their emotions. There are so many things to organise, so many personas to play.

But then Rachael adds, 'It must have been terrible for you because I know how concerned you were for Cassie's well-being, always.' She looks up at me and will not look away.

I, in turn, regard this woman, and suddenly I think, *She understands me, she understands me as nobody before ever has.* For a moment I have a terrible urge; an urge to open myself to her. Never before have I felt the pressing desire to share my innermost thoughts. I almost shudder. I have searched for a person to understand me for a long time. Once, a person like Rachael might have made a difference to me and to the life I have chosen. Someone like Rachael could have been my sounding-board, could perhaps have held me back from the dangerous currents of my impetuousness.

Now, of course, it is too late. This woman is dangerous; perhaps the most dangerous person I know. She understands me too well. I don't go near Rachael for the rest of the morning, but sometimes I catch her looking at me sideways, out of lowered lids. I realise that I will have to act, today.

I bide my time until I see Rachael packing up to leave and then I approach Odette. I am as hypnotic as a snake: one warm hand is placed on her arm, my eyes lock with hers. I am wide-eyed, upset and appalled. 'Odette, something has happened and I don't know if I should tell May or not.'

Odette leans forward, she cannot help herself, she is mesmerised by the potential for poison gossip. 'What is it?' She is heavily pregnant and we are so close that her stomach presses into me. I can feel the bulge of her belly button like a warm slug; I steel myself not to pull away from her.

'I was just in the garden and I saw Rachael...' I shake my head and Odette's moves with me. 'Oh look, perhaps I shouldn't say anything...' I lower my hand from Odette's arm.

'No! Tell me ... What happened?' Odette is leaning further forward as I sway slightly back. Her eyes do not leave mine.

'It's only that she hit James, hard. It's left quite a red mark.'

Odette brings one ring-encrusted hand to her mouth, leans back slightly. 'How dreadful!'

'Well, I suppose she had cause ... James had just pushed Tamara.'

'Was Tamara hurt?' Odette leans forward again, we are doing the dance of the cobra.

'No,' I reply, 'she didn't seem to be, but still, James shouldn't have pushed her.'

'I know, but Rachael had no right to hit James. That's terrible.' Odette is shaking her head in disbelief. Her body sways with indignation. 'I mean, no one has the right to hit someone else's child.'

I avert my eyes. 'Well... James is pretty naughty.'

'No,' Odette is quite convinced, 'it doesn't matter. Rachael shouldn't have hit him. She should have told May, not hit him.'

'Mmmm, maybe you're right, Odette. Rachael can be a bit quick sometimes.'

Now Odette is nodding righteously. 'Exactly, I agree. She lost her temper with Chris once. He did some little thing. She *has* got a bad temper, you know.'

'Oh yes, I know,' I agree – must agree. She is, after all, saying the things I want her to say.

'Look,' I lean forward as if to whisper. 'I think it's best if we don't tell May. It'll only upset her.'

'No, I don't agree.' Enthralled and empowered by her knowledge, Odette is decisive. 'I think that May should be told. If you don't want to do it, I will. I don't mind.'

'Oh I don't know, Odette, I feel a bit bad about this.'

'I won't tell her who told me, okay?' I nod, yes. Odette's proposal is really more than okay.

Odette glances around the room. 'I'll just wait until Rachael leaves before I say anything.' Odette is not, after all, completely stupid.

As I prepare to leave I notice that there is a lot of whispering going on. Across the room I see May sitting on the couch with Odette. She looks pale and shocked; on her lap is James. High on his thigh the outline of a red hand mark can still be seen.

I smile to myself. Rachael's act of betrayal will not go unpunished. There will not be any direct confrontation, of course. That would be too upsetting for all involved. No, ostracism will be sufficient for these women; after all, why give Rachael the chance to defend herself? Gradually she will be excluded. Soon enough she will get the hint. She will find other activities with which to fill her life, activities outside my social orbit. It has been a good morning's work, I think to myself. That'll teach Rachael to cross me; that'll teach *anyone* to cross me.

It is only when I am halfway home that I allow myself to laugh. *I enjoyed that*, I think. I'm not sure which was more satisfying: hitting that little shit

James, or so cleverly manipulating Odette to achieve what I wanted. Who would have thought such a silly trick would have worked so effectively?

What I have done is so funny that my eyes stream with tears of laughter. I can see Zach in the rear-vision mirror. He is looking at me as if I have gone mad. That idea makes me laugh even more. He has no way of knowing what his mother has become: first a murderer and now a liar. It all seems so terribly funny.

TWENTY

*I*t is a long, hot summer. I take Zach to the park often. It is down a steep hill. Zach rides in a baby carrier on my back. He sits straight-backed stretching high; he is desperate to see as much as he can. Zach loves it when we run down the hill to the park. He giggles and throws his hands around. His wispy blond hair floats up and down in the puffs of air.

The walking does me good. I lose weight. Old clothes fit. I change my hairstyle. It is very short and black. Daniel likes it. He runs his hands over my scalp until my hair stands up in spikes. We both laugh. It is good to hear him laugh again.

I meet new people in the park, people who do not know that I was ever mother to a daughter named Cassie, a daughter who did not like to sleep and who threw her legs around in anger.

Now I have only one child to wake me at night, and Daniel has agreed to move Zach out of our room, provided the baby monitor is turned up to full volume. Finally the cloud of fatigue which I have worn for months does not lie as heavily. I can think again. Daniel and I have begun to have regular sex and one night towards the end of summer he says to me, 'I think we should have another one.'

In my post-orgasmic glow I am not sure what he is talking about. Another what, another session? I don't answer, so he clarifies: 'Another child.'

I am horrified, too horrified to speak. Does he not realise that my life is just settling down again, that for the first time in months I can read a few pages of a book without my mind wandering, that toys no longer litter the hallway, that we are having sex again? For God's sake, does he want to jeopardise all of this?

I find my tongue. 'It's too soon, Daniel. I can't do it, not just yet.'

'But you seem to be coping so well. It seems to me as if this might be the next step that we both need.'

'Appearances aren't everything,' I reply cautiously. 'I'm scared, Daniel. I'm just very scared to have another baby.'

Daniel persists. 'Maybe there's someone you could talk to about this. I know you don't want to see a counsellor, but what about an old friend? Someone like Maureen? She might be good for you. You know, someone you can talk to, open up to. It was very nice of her to come to the funeral and she seems to be someone who can... I don't know...give comfort or something.'

Daniel's tone is casual, too casual; I have not forgotten the funeral clinch.

So, I think, *you suppose Maureen would be good for me, good to convince me to have more children, good to convince me that I'm happy in the suburbs, that it's okay to become what she has become, it's all right to turn into everything I despise. But if you think I am about to let that happen then you are sadly mistaken.*

'So,' I say, 'you were thinking that Maureen, with her sympathetic ear, might be able to convince me that rushing out and having another child is the right thing to do.'

'No, not that.' Daniel sounds exasperated. 'I was thinking she might be able to help you. She's very emotionally honest. You might enjoy spending time with someone like that.'

'No, Daniel, I wouldn't. There are things I would like to do, but spending time with Maureen is not one of them. Maybe you're the one who's really keen to spend time with Maureen and her precious "emotional honesty".'

'Be reasonable, sweetheart. All I want is for you and Zach to be all right and for us to have another child. We're not getting any younger, you know.'

He's right. We aren't. My body is older; it wouldn't recover as well. Zach is almost walking; he is becoming more independent. I would have to begin again. My heart hammers. I clench my fists in agitation. Heat spots rise in my face. I turn away from Daniel. I don't want him to read my betraying body.

Daniel misunderstands the movement. It is better that he does. He drags his finger down my spine and rests it in one of the dimples above my bottom.

'We know that the odds of something like Cassie's death happening again are so low as to be almost nonexistent.'

He sounds like a textbook, but I know he is desperate for me to agree with him. He is desperate to return us to what we were – a perfect nuclear family. Can he not see how dangerous that would be? It would be dangerous for us, dangerous for Zach, dangerous for any new child.

I reach around and grab his hand, pulling him closer to me. I am beginning to calm my renegade body. The control is returning.

'Oh Daniel, I love you. You know that I do, but I can't do it again...' I choose to leave the door open a little, '...just yet.'

Daniel is crying. 'I loved her so much. And we live with her death every day. It's not only what she was, it's what she would have become. It's the useless waste of her death that I hate so much.'

I cuddle him hard and say, 'Remember what you said at the funeral – we were lucky to have her as long as we did. Some things aren't meant to last.'

Daniel grunts. 'You're always telling me to move on. Well, that's what I'm *trying* to do, move on.'

'I'm not ready to move on to another baby,' I say. I will not continue down that path any further. Daniel hears it in my voice and understands. It makes him angry.

'Fuck it! Why will you never discuss this properly? You close the fucking shutters and that's it, end of conversation, nobody home.'

'Don't ever speak to me in that way,' I say. 'Don't ever take it out on me. You're not the only one hurt by this.'

'By what?' He is almost shouting. 'By what? Why will you never say it? By the senseless, useless death of our beautiful daughter, our Cassie. Why can you never refer directly to her death?'

Again I turn away from Daniel. I will not respond to his anger and he realises that. The fact that he is angry now is a sign of his desperation, but I will not let him know that I understand. It is important that I maintain some power.

I close my eyes. The conversation is over. Daniel picks up his pillow. He will spend the night on the sofa.

I am awake for a long time that night. It is difficult for me to control my breathing. *Nothing has changed,* I am thinking. *Everything that I have done for Daniel so that he and I could begin to live again has come to nothing. I'm still a mother, he a father. True, I am not as tired as when Cassie was alive, but we still don't go out together; we still haven't learned to live again. Now Daniel wants to drag me back to what I was, a barely functioning machine, a mother who dwelt only in the half light of other people's needs.*

It is unfair of Daniel to put such pressure upon me. Not only do I understand the danger of what he is asking, but I understand more than that. I know, even if Daniel is unwilling or unable to acknowledge it, I know that I have barely begun to live.

TWENTY-ONE

$\mathcal{T}$he next week I find an advertisement in the paper:

ADVERTISING

We are an award-winning, full-service, boutique design and advertising agency.

We provide our clients with high-quality solutions ranging from marketing communications and brand advertising to direct marketing and design.

We have a dynamic culture in which the team works hard, achieves results and has fun.

You will have a solid background at Account Director level in a mid to large-sized agency.

You will possess energy, initiative and a burning
    desire to add value to your clients' businesses.
You will work closely with the creative team to
    develop innovative advertising and media
    solutions which are sensitive to your clients'
    needs.

I have heard of the company: it is only a few years old with a reputation for being progressive. I know that it has already won a couple of awards, including a Cannes Cyber Lion for online advertising.

While the pay level is slightly below what I was on before leaving work to have Cassie, what interests me most about the position is the scope it might present. In small, dynamic companies, power bases are constantly shifting, new opportunities arise all the time. I am particularly excited by the fact I would be working closely with the creative team. I have a very strong creative streak which was not allowed expression in my previous workplace with its rigid, old-fashioned division between the account and creative sides of the business.

I decide to send in an application.

For the next few days I am busy. From the back of the filing cabinet I pull out my old résumés and letters. I buy a book on job application and interview techniques. I search the internet for tips on securing a job. I have been out of the workforce for over two years; I know how quickly things can change. It is important that my application is up-to-date and relevant. I will *not* make a fool of myself.

When I am ready to write I put away everything I have read and sit before the blank screen of the computer. I have thought carefully about how I wish to present myself. I am ready to become the person for which the company is searching. For the next three nights, in the time between Zach going to bed and Daniel coming home, I create and re-create, buff and polish. In lines of text I represent myself as a competent, dedicated employee able to work to direction and tight deadlines, capable of building and maintaining strong client relationships, but with a creative flair which can be called upon if necessary. It is myself as I am capable of being – if I get the job, of course.

Finally I am finished. All my effort has resulted in two flimsy pieces of printed paper upon which my future rests. For as I have created, the yearning within me has grown. I know that I want this job. Not only is it a connection to my old life, but it will hold at bay Daniel and his demands for another child.

I send in the application.

Ten days later I am on my way to the interview. I have enough warning to arrange care for Zach and to have my hair trimmed and recoloured. I do not have enough time to buy a new outfit. An old, almost fashionable black suit, that was squeezed, forgotten, into my side of the wardrobe, has to do.

The firm's offices are on the edge of the city. For many years this area was a slum. Now it is revitalised. Red brick buildings with iron grids on the windows have been replaced by reflective high rises with fancy names and heavy-set doormen. Slick women with expensive blunt-cut hairstyles and designer shoes cruise the sidewalk. The men are groomed and exercised. They look as if they have stepped out of the pages of a glossy magazine. There is a vibe in the air. This is where it is all happening. Suddenly I feel hungry for it. Hungry for the artifice and pretence, hungry for the energy that is bouncing from person to person, hungry for the feeling that this is the centre. God, how I have missed this, trapped in my suburban haven; God, how I have missed the power of it all.

I wriggle in my uncomfortable suit. I look around my car, at the greasy fingermarks on my back window, at the half-chewed rusks that have been thrown on the floor. I know with certainty that this is not what I want.

Suddenly I hear my mother's voice. It comes at me from the depth of a nightmare. '*Stay in your room until I call you. I don't want to see your face until then.*' Next, a male voice. '*Where's your daughter?*' And my mother replying. '*At a friend's place. We have the night to ourselves, just you and me.*' *That night I am too afraid to leave the room. I pee in a cup I have near the bed and pour it silently out the window. I don't leave the room until morning when my mother greets me and cooks a breakfast that I am unable to eat.* It's not my fault, I tell myself; the women in my family have never been good mothers. Why has Daniel failed to see this? Why is he so desperate for me to be something I am not?

Today I am lucky with parking, pulling up right outside the address I have been given. It is a post-modern building that, from the street, looks unstable.

Like one of Escher's drawings, I imagine it to be full of impossible spaces and infinitely looping stairs – leading to nowhere except themselves. I wonder if, once inside, I will ever be able to find my way out again.

Inside, the building is so new that I can smell the fresh paint, the glue rising from the carpet. Signs are still being erected. Everything is clean and untainted. Many of the offices are unoccupied. They stand open and expectant at the promise of what they may become.

The firm I seek occupies one of the uppermost floors of the building. As I make my way there I realise I am not nervous. I feel like a thoroughbred whose best race is still to come. Adrenaline is a powerful beast which I have long ago learned to tame and ride. It will carry me through today. Of that I have no doubt.

The interviewer and company principal, Mr Drake, sits behind a huge desk, rising to shake my hand as I enter. He directs me to a seat near a small table in the corner of the room and, picking up a pad and pen, joins me.

There is no preamble; Drake moves right to the point. 'Your credentials certainly look good.

A Bachelor of Communications, several years in a large advertising firm at the same level as that advertised.' He looks up. The world is reflected in his glasses. I see myself, hands clasped and resting on the table, face suitably alert and agreeable. I see the door behind me and, at an angle, distorted, I can glimpse the next-door office tower. 'But you've been out of the industry for a couple of years.'

He stops for a moment. I refuse to step into the silence just yet; let him finish what he has to say, let him fully expose his concerns. 'So what makes you think you can do this? We have younger people applying for this job, people with more recent degrees, more relevant job experience.'

I had not expected him to be quite so direct, but I know that I can answer his concerns.

I uncross my legs and lean forward. 'I know what I want, Mr Drake. I'm hungry for this type of work. I can guarantee that none of the other applicants will have my hunger. On top of that I am eminently qualified. I graduated at the top of my class in over seventy per cent of the subjects I studied at university. During my years in the industry I brought millions of dollars worth of advertising revenue to the companies I worked for. I captured clients whose advertising campaigns gained international recognition. I can give you a list of referees to contact. I am thorough, meticulous and disciplined with an unerring eye for detail. I assure you, no one else of my calibre will apply for this job.'

I can see that he is taken aback by my response. I know that not all I have told him is reflected in my résumé. I learned this trick many years ago. The application should contain merely enough information to get you to an interview, nothing more; you leave something up your sleeve for later. Something to surprise people, to put them on the back foot. Then you have won...and with Drake's next words I know I have.

'Why are you interested in working for this company then, why us? Why not try for a job with the organisations you have worked for in the past?'

'You're new on the scene,' I reply, 'with a reputation for being progressive and dynamic. I'm no longer interested in working for large companies that provide no flexibility. I realise that I'll be starting at a lower pay level than when I left the industry. But you'll get value for money out of me. I promise you that.'

I am not surprised when Drake rings the next day to offer me the job. He would like me to start in two weeks. I am cautiously excited. After all, I still have Daniel to deal with.

TWENTY-TWO

That night, Daniel and I are washing up when I begin. I am so casual that you would never believe my heart is racing.

'Daniel, I've been giving some thought to the things you suggested – you know, about talking to someone and having another baby. I'm sorry, darling, but I'm just not ready for another child yet. I'm just not. And as much as I like Maureen, and I know that you do too, she's part of my past. I need more than that. I need something to take me into the future. You have your work. You're out there every day. You have people and things that give you something else to think about. I have nothing. I'm here every day with Zach and the memories.' My eyes are downcast; it appears as if I may be about to cry.

Daniel places his soapy hands on my shoulders. I feel the wet seep through my shirt. He pulls me to him. 'I know how hard this is. That's why I think you need to talk to someone about it, about what's happened to us. Anybody, it doesn't have to be Maureen. Anybody you can trust.'

I burrow my head into Daniel's chest. 'Oh Daniel. I know. I know that you only want what's best for us, but I don't think that just talking to someone is going to help.'

'Come on, come over here.' Daniel shepherds me to the couch. 'The washing-up can wait. It's really important that we talk about this. I've been wanting to have a conversation like this for weeks.' He settles a cushion behind my back. 'So what is there,' he asks, 'what is there that you think would help? I would do anything to help us move on.'

'Well...' I hesitate as if afraid to proceed.

'Yes,' says Daniel. He uses the voice he usually reserves for Zach. Soft and low. 'Yes, tell me. I really, truly want to know.'

'Well, I had a phone call yesterday. An ex-work colleague heard about this job that was going and she thought I might be interested so she passed my contact details on and a...' I hesitate a moment as if unable to remember the details, '...a Mr Drake rang. He's looking at expanding his advertising agency. He's on the search for good people...and he thought I might be interested.'

'You?' Daniel sounds dumbfounded. Obviously, this conversation is not proceeding as he'd envisaged. I almost laugh. Some things are too easy.

'Oh Daniel,' I chide, 'is that so hard to believe? I was good, you know. People still remember me. This isn't the first job offer I've had.'

'It isn't?'

'No, it's not. I just haven't told you before, that's all, because I haven't been interested. But Daniel, I really feel as if this is the right thing for me. I'm stuck you see. I'm in a loop. I can't go back and I'm too scared to go forward. I just *can't* contemplate having another child while I'm in this state.'

'No, I can see that,' says Daniel. There is old sadness in his voice. 'I just can't see, can't believe, that you going back to work is the right thing for us.'

It's always 'us', I think, *always us*. It's never enough for Daniel that sometimes it should be 'me'.

Ever since the children were born I have not been a 'me', I have been an 'us'. I am so sick of it.

'But Daniel, I want this. I need this.'

'So what are you suggesting? That you go back to work full-time?' Daniel is shaking his head, 'Because I can't, I simply can't agree to that.'

'Oh Daniel,' I wipe my eyes. 'You know what advertising agencies are like, they need me there full-time.'

'No.' Daniel places his hand on my shoulder. 'I'm sorry sweetheart, but if this... Drake person won't let you work part-time, then you will have to find somewhere that will.' He is shaking his head, a small frown on his face.

I see that Daniel will not budge on this point. But he *has* implicitly agreed to my return to work; at least I have that to build on.

'And what about Zach?' Daniel asks now.

I am ready for this one. 'I've thought about that,' I reply. 'Apparently a new child-care centre has opened down near the park. They still have some vacancies. They're supposed to be very good...maybe I could ring them tomorrow, arrange a time for us to go and have a look... What do you think?'

Daniel nods slowly, reluctantly, '*If* this child-care centre is any good, and *if* you can get part-time work...maybe we can look at this a bit more seriously.'

And then Daniel is hugging me, pulling me towards him. I know that my returning to work is not what he wants, but he has told me that he would do anything to help me move on, *anything*. 'Are you sure,' he asks – his mouth buried in my hair, 'are you really sure that this will help us pull together as a family again?'

I nod as much as I am able. 'I'm sure, Daniel; I'm really, really sure.'

TWENTY-THREE

I start work. I love it from the moment I walk in. The vibe is back. I have on new clothes. I have even pulled out my old make-up bag and used one of my twenty eyeshadow colours. *Watch out world*, I want to scream. *Watch out, I'm back.*

The first couple of days I set up meetings with some corporations that were former clients of mine. I know that winning their work for Drake's agency will be a real coup for me. I am excited about the prospects which this job has given me.

Drake has agreed to me working part-time for the first few weeks. *To ease myself back into the workforce*, I tell him. I have, of course, not told Daniel that this part-time arrangement is only temporary. I hope that when he sees how much happier I am at work he will understand that working full-time will be a far better arrangement for me.

The centre where Zach is in care rings me at eleven. He has not stopped crying since I left. The staff are concerned that he may be coming down with something. I tell them I will pick him up as soon as possible.

At five-thirty I arrive at the centre. Zach's eyes are puffy and when he sees me he clings to me as if he never wants to let go. That night he wakes up five times; each time he is screaming for me and I am the only one who can comfort him and rock him back to sleep. By the next morning I am exhausted, but desperate to go to work. Daniel offers to drop Zach off at the centre and to pick him up. Thankfully, I agree.

At lunchtime the phone rings. It is Daniel. 'I'm home with Zach. He couldn't settle. They told me it happened yesterday as well and that you didn't pick him up until late afternoon.'

'Look Daniel,' I reply, 'I picked Zach up as quickly as I could. There were just things that had to be done.'

That night Zach has a fever. I put him to bed and come out to the cold stare of Daniel.

'He's sick. You left him in a child-care centre when he was clearly upset and now he's sick.'

'Children get sick all the time,' I reply. 'Especially when they've just been exposed to a whole new set of kids.' I will not bear the brunt of Daniel's anger. My mother used to get angry with me when I was a child. No one is allowed to talk to me that way anymore.

'Look,' says Daniel, 'I understand that you feel you need to work and I understand that in the first few weeks things can be difficult – you're on trial, you need to work hard – but I think it's important that Zach is picked up from the child-care centre by five at the latest.'

I snort. 'There's no way I can get away from work every afternoon by four-thirty, especially since I'm only working three days a week anyway, you know that.'

'Yes,' says Daniel, 'I do know that so I'm not asking you to. What I am suggesting is that we share the job. One afternoon a week you pick him up early and I'll do it the other two afternoons. The next week we alternate.'

'Yeah right,' I say. 'As if your company will let you get home that early.'

'They have no choice. They'll have to agree to it, or I'll leave.'

I roll my eyes heavenward. I have never heard Daniel be more ridiculous.

'How could we afford that? We wouldn't be able to make the repayments on the house if you did something that stupid.'

'I don't think you understand.' Daniel is tense and stiff; he is barely breathing. 'My family comes before anything. Zach is the only child I have left. The company will let me do this; they will have to let me do this. I'll do some work from home in the evenings if necessary, but they will agree to this. Now you need to find out if your company will agree as well.'

I shake my head. 'For God's sake, Daniel. Zach will get used to child care. There are numerous studies showing high-quality child care is actually good for children. Most kids just take a bit of time to settle in.'

'He's not "most kids" he's our kid. I don't want him in child care any longer than is absolutely necessary. We need to try this. I insist that we try this.'

I am speechless at Daniel's request. Even if his company lets him knock off early one or two afternoons a week, what about me? I have just started work again. I haven't yet proved myself. I am working on a part-time basis which Drake expects me to up to full-time sooner rather than later, and I cannot imagine a request to leave early on a regular basis being met favourably at all. But I know Daniel. He is easygoing to a point. And once that point is reached he is a prize bull. I know he will not back down on this.

'Okay,' I nod. 'I'll ask. I'll see what I can do.' Already I am beginning to plan how I can manage the situation.

Daniel decides to take the last three days of the following week off to care for Zach while I work. To give me time to settle in, he says; to give me time to request some early afternoons.

Each night over those few days I arrive home to find Daniel and Zach playing together in the lounge.

One night it is trains, another it is puzzles. Daniel dotes on Zach now. There is no other word for it. When they are together Zach giggles like a breathless steam engine. So engrossed are they in each other that it can take some time for them even to realise that I am home, standing, watching them.

On Friday night Zach staggers over to me and buries his head in my knees. Daniel gives me a brush on the cheek. He has barely touched me all week.

I find myself speaking. 'I talked to Drake; he understands that I'll have to leave early one or two afternoons a week. He says he can live with it.'

Daniel nods. 'Okay, it should be fine from my end as well. Les's not happy about it, but we agreed to give it a trial for a few weeks and see how it pans out. So long as my work doesn't suffer it should be okay.'

Daniel leans over and kisses me properly. 'Thank you for all you've done in this. I know how much work means to you.'

He really has no idea.

For two weeks we go about our arrangements. I work long days when I don't have to pick Zach up, and slip out from work early – without telling anyone – on the days that I do have to. With the slightly shorter time in child care, Zach seems to have settled in quite well. I am hoping that in a couple of weeks – with a happier Zach to dangle in front of Daniel – he will agree to me working my full required hours *and* increasing my days at work; Drake is growing impatient for me to move to a full-time basis as promised. *Maybe I can make this succeed*, I think, *maybe*.

It's a Wednesday. It was Daniel's day for picking up Zach; I have come home late to a dark, seemingly empty house. Where is Daniel? Even the television isn't on. I discard my bag and shoes and make my way to the lounge-room. Daniel has dragged a chair to the window overlooking the back garden. His back is to me. All I can see clearly is his head silhouetted against the last of the light.

'Hello,' I say.

'When were you going to tell me?' he asks.

I stop mid-inhalation. My breath is frozen, an icicle inside my throat.

'Tell you what?' I play for time; I have some inkling of what may be coming, but I am not sure.

'I called your office about twenty minutes ago. I wanted to catch you before you left work. I only wanted you to pick up a loaf of bread on the way home. That's all, just a loaf of bread.'

I am quite sure that the dark house and Daniel's back are due to more than a loaf of bread. I am silent until he continues.

'Drake answered the phone. He said you'd just left. I thanked him, like a fool I thanked him for agreeing to you going part-time and for letting you come home early one or two afternoons a week. Guess what he said?'

Still I remain silent.

'He said that he'd never agreed to any such thing; that you'd never come to him with a request for shorter afternoons and that you promised him you'd up your hours to full-time gradually over the next few weeks. And Drake told me one more thing, one more very interesting thing.' Daniel still hasn't turned to face me.

'What was it Daniel?'

'He told me that at your interview he spelled out very clearly that you would be expected to work long hours. That they were a small, boutique company, that they couldn't afford to employ anyone who would fail to pull their weight.'

Now Daniel turns to look at me and I wish that he hadn't. His eyes are vacant. He has not been crying, I can tell that, but I have no idea what is going on in his head. It is the first time this has happened. 'You lied to me when you agreed to go back to work on a part-time basis *and* you lied to me even before that: you very specifically told me that you were offered that job on the basis of your work history, that you hadn't even had to go through a job interview, that you hadn't had to write a job application. Well, look what I found on the computer.' He holds up two pieces of paper, my job application.

It is the written word held up to condemn me. Anything else I might have been able to deny, but not that. I blurt out the first stupid words that come to mind: 'How did you get hold of that? I deleted it.'

Daniel snorts, 'You're not as clever as you think, are you? The recycle bin hadn't been emptied. A simple, stupid mistake.' There is silence as he breathes, as I breathe, the same air, but a galaxy apart.

'You know,' says Daniel, 'all I wanted was for you to be happy, for Zach to be happy, for us to be a real family again. And all I've got from you are lies – lies and deception. You've disregarded all the things that are really, truly important to me. You've torn them up like tissue paper and held them to the breeze.'

'Oh Daniel.' I sink down beside his chair. 'Oh Daniel. I'm sorry, so sorry. I didn't tell you about the interview because I was scared you'd be angry if you knew I'd gone looking for a job. And I kept quiet about Drake's preference that I build my hours up to a full-time basis because I was afraid that you wouldn't agree to me working. But really Daniel I did it all for the family. I looked for a good job so I could put Cassie's death behind me, so I could be a good wife again, a good mother again.'

'How can you say that? You've hurt the family, you've hurt me, you've hurt Zach. He's the one you really need to apologise to, not me. How long did you think you could keep all this going, all this lying?'

'Oh Daniel, I knew that Drake wouldn't take me on if I couldn't work full-time. And then I was sure if I almost immediately asked for early afternoons once or twice a week it would mean the end of my job there. I *need* that job, Daniel. I need it, to get better, to be able to move on. I thought, maybe, maybe this week I'd talk to Drake about the possibility of staying on as a part-time employee on an indefinite basis. Drake knows my work now, he likes it; I think that he'll agree to my requests. I just needed some time to prove myself.'

'Prove yourself! At the expense of everything. At the expense of telling the truth to me. At the expense of being there for your son. That's not good enough and you know it!' Daniel is angry, intractable.

I am so desperate to cling to my hard-won freedom that I start to cry. I have never tried this with Daniel before, but I have seen it work for other people. I dissolve in a heart-wrenching heap on the floor. The tears flow effortlessly.

Daniel cries as well. I move over to him and sink my head onto his lap. We cry in harmony. Finally, he speaks.

'Look, just tell me what you want. You want to work full-time and for me to stay home? Fine, I'll do that, but please don't punish Zach for your desire to work.'

Daniel's suggestion takes me by surprise. Surely he is bluffing. We could never keep the house on my salary alone. His real agenda is obviously to force me to stop work. It has been his agenda from the start. Daniel has never appreciated all that I have done for him. He is selfish and ungrateful. I wonder why I have not previously seen this.

Daniel speaks again. 'Anyway, we can talk about it this weekend, I've asked your mother to come over and care for Zach.'

'My mother?'

'I've booked a couple of nights in the mountains. We need time to talk, to sort this thing out, and I don't want to do it here. There are too many memories in this house. I want us to get away. I don't expect the weekend to be a pleasant or easy one. But it's something we need to do. It's something I need to do.'

'And you're willing to leave my mother to care for Zach while we go away?'

'I am. This is important and your mother loves Zach. She's part of the family. I trust her. She'll take good care of him.'

I allow all this to sink in. A couple of nights in the mountains would be nice. Even if I have to see my mother to be able to do it. How typical, I am able to think, that my mother should have the opportunity to view another important moment in my life, headlined something like 'The year my marriage reached crisis point'. I try not to laugh out loud because it is, of course, inappropriate to share this thought with Daniel at this point, so I don't.

TWENTY-FOUR

My mother arrives fashionably late at six-thirty when Daniel had asked her to be at our place at six. She is, if at all possible, skinnier than ever, as her ludicrously short skirt reveals only too clearly. She air-kisses me as she minces through the door followed by a cloud of perfume which will no doubt make Zach gag when she bathes and feeds him.

I show my mother Zach's carefully arranged food in the fridge, enough for every meal while we are away. I also show her a selection of frozen meals for herself. She nods absently at this. They won't be eaten, I know, but I have done my duty as a host. She waits until the end of the tour to rub it in.

'You know, darling, how delighted I am to be able to help you out like this. I know how independent you and Daniel like to be, but, really, who better to call on in this time of need than your own mother.'

Yes, my mother. The woman who, when I was three, locked me in my bedroom so that I wouldn't wake her at night; who put me on my first diet at seven; and who, when I was fifteen, tried to steal my first boyfriend. I know how desperate Daniel is for us to have this weekend away together, so I will not allow myself to be antagonised by her. Instead, I nod sweetly. Daniel has obviously told her too much.

My mother and Zach stand outside to farewell us as we drive away. Zach has one little fist raised and he is clenching and unclenching it in his version of waving. He is teary. His bottom lip quivers, and his nose starts to twitch, but I'm sure that he'll be okay. Children are amazingly resilient. We wave and blow kisses until we are at the bottom of the driveway and then we are away.

This is the first time that Daniel and I have gone away together since Cassie was born. It'll be the first time since the children were born that I will sleep under a roof which doesn't shelter at least one of them. Such freedom! Despite the issues that remain to be resolved between Daniel and myself, I know that I will enjoy this weekend. Finally we are doing something for ourselves. I am so happy to be leaving the house, that I'm sure I'll be able to face anything Daniel might throw at me. After all, he can't exactly forbid me to work. And I know that the further we move away from suburbia and my role of 'mother', the more power I will have over him.

Daniel has told me that we are going to the mountains, but he has not told me where we are staying. This omission makes the trip even more exciting. We spent the first few days of our honeymoon up here. It was winter; at one stage it snowed. Flakes of shaved ice piled against our door, tumbling over the threshold when we dared to venture out. It was a wonderland. I had never seen anything more beautiful.

It is after ten when we begin to descend a long driveway to our mountain hideaway. I lost my bearings nearly an hour ago. We are further into the mountains than I have ever been. We are driving over gravel now and the sound of the crunching echoes around the car, too loud for conversation. It doesn't matter anyway, we have not spoken much during this trip. It's the way we both want it. The ride here has given us a chance to shed our skins, to become once more the people we were, before I gave up my career, before we had children, before one of those children died. I can feel my old self, my old confidence reasserting itself.

The headlights of the car suddenly illuminate a sign showing the name of our destination, *Mountain View*. I have heard of this place, have read about it in lifestyle magazines. It is expensive and exclusive. I am impressed that Daniel was able to book here on such short notice; I am impressed that he feels we can afford to stay here; I am impressed because his choice of accommodation reflects the obvious importance he attaches to saving our marriage, to bridging our impasse.

As if reading my mind, Daniel breaks the silence that the halting of the car has brought.

'They had a vacancy. We were lucky. And I thought that anything less than somewhere like this would be a compromise.' He turns to face me and takes one of my hands in his. 'I'm determined to work our way through this. I'm determined to reach an outcome with which we can all live.'

His words are solemn. Daniel has always taken things seriously. He approaches any problem, even personal ones, as if it is a puzzle needing a solution.

'We will, darling, we will,' I reply. I lean over to kiss him. He smells tired and slightly sick. It is evidence of what these last eight months have taken out of him.

Our room is beautifully appointed, the spa-bath deep, the bed exquisitely comfortable. I sleep the sleep of the dead, or the innocent. I do not dream. I wake before Daniel and observe him while he sleeps. He is restless. His eyelids flicker. His hands clench and unclench. He seems to be running a marathon in his sleep and when he finally wakes, there are deep black circles under his eyes.

Daniel has planned a hike for the morning. The hotel has packed a picnic lunch and Daniel puts it in his backpack. This walk will not be anything too strenuous. We will make our way over a small rise known as the Devil's Hump, and then along the valley floor before making a steep, but short ascent of the other side to a viewing platform which, according to the guidebook, promises 'a panoramic view of the five pillars'.

It is overcast and the sun hangs low in a beaten pewter sky as we set out. We have not yet spoken about the issues which we have come here to resolve. I have determined that I will not be the one to raise them. There is power in knowing your enemy, but not being the first to strike. I am languid and relaxed, a lioness in her prime. It will take a lot to defeat me.

As the path narrows I am content to follow Daniel, keeping up with his steady, insistent pace. I count my footsteps, five hundred and nine, five hundred and ten, five hundred and eleven. My mind echoes with the beat, nothing more. By ten-thirty, flies have settled on the slight dampness of Daniel's shoulders. We are about three-quarters of the way along the valley floor when Daniel calls a halt. We find a spot, a grotto, perhaps. The rocks are damp as if perpetually watered by a hidden spring. We perch: me on one rock; Daniel on another. Daniel swings his pack to the ground and passes me a water bottle. I drink deeply, counting my gulps. The water tastes like canvas. It reminds me of a camping trip

I took with my parents before my father died. It was winter and there were no showers, only a river, which flowed so slowly that it was covered in lilypads. We didn't bathe in three days. My mother declared that she 'would never do that again'. My father and I laughed at her discomfort.

When I stop drinking I find that Daniel is looking at me.

'Good?'

I nod. It is good. Good to drink, good to be here with him, good not to have to worry about changing nappies or preparing baby food.

'Are you happy?' I ask him suddenly.

'Happy?' He rolls the question around in his mouth. 'Happy to be here with you. But everything I do now echoes with her.'

I don't ask who 'her' is. I know: my daughter, our daughter. My forever rival for his affections.

I wipe the sweat from my forehead. 'Yes, I know how it is for you.' My reply is too short and sounds too much of accusation. I realise it as soon as the words are out of my mouth.

His grey eyes look steadily at me. 'But not for you.' Is it a question? I'm not sure, but I will treat it as such.

'Of course it is for me. Of course I miss her. Of course I think about her all the time.' Even to my ears it sounds like a well-rehearsed litany.

Daniel leans towards me. 'Do you? I wonder. I wonder. I've been wondering a lot over the last few days.' His voice trails off and he looks into the middle distance.

My heart has grown cold. What is he getting at?

Daniel continues. 'I've done a lot of reading about infant death recently. As Doctor Hadid told us, the chance of a child Cassie's age dying from an unexplained cause is very small.'

My hand has begun to move without my control. I realise that I am tearing at the moss that covers most of my rock, ripping it from its mooring. With difficulty I gain some control. Daniel is being unfair. This line of discussion is not what I had expected.

'Yes, of course I know that,' I reply. 'I've read about it as well. That's why it's so dreadfully difficult to believe that it happened to our family.'

'So you've been reading? I thought you'd dealt with it all by putting everything behind you. That's what I told Cindy.'

'Cindy?' He is taking me down pathways for which I am unprepared.

'Mmmmm, Cindy.'

'Who's Cindy?' If he is seeking my attention, he now has it. My hands are firmly in my lap.

'Cindy's the counsellor from the hospital, the one you would never agree to talk to.'

Shit! Cindy. I remember now. She'd rung me several times in the weeks after Cassie's death. I'd never responded to her and finally she'd seemed to realise that I didn't welcome her attentions.

'I spoke to Cindy on Thursday. I wanted to know what a normal grieving process for a mother might be. I was hoping even now to find some way to help you, to help us. Cindy said there was really no normal pattern, but that it was usually the mother who – externally at least – took these things the hardest, who often blamed herself for the death of her child. She said that sadness and guilt could manifest in many different ways – maybe a morbid fear for your other children; maybe an intense sense of culpability, such as blaming yourself and questioning your actions in the lead-up to the child's death. What Cindy said got me thinking and I realised that you've never exhibited any of the classic signs of grief. Maybe someone who didn't know you well wouldn't have realised, but I know you well, very well. You haven't changed, you haven't reacted. You haven't wanted to talk to anybody, to confide in anybody – not me, not Cindy, not Maureen, nobody. You've carried on your life exactly as if Cassie had never existed.'

There is silence. In the distance I hear the cry of a solitary crow.

'What do you think all this means?' Daniel looks directly at me. Unfortunately this is a question for which he requires a real answer.

'Daniel, I don't handle things like other people, you know that. You said it was one of the reasons you loved me, one of the reasons you asked me to marry you. Why should I exhibit these classic signs of grief? They're classic because that's what the majority of people do. Why should I be the same as everybody else? Surely you're not going to punish me for not mourning like an automaton!'

'Not an automaton,' he fires back. 'Like a human. Like a mother. Like someone who cared about whether our daughter lived or died. I know that you don't always handle things like other people and that's why I've been so patient. I was sure that one day the dam wall would break and you would finally reveal the full extent of your grief. But it hasn't happened. And you know what? Now that I've learned how easy you find it to lie to me, now that I've discovered how easy you find it to turn your back on Zach, I've been wondering...'

Fuck, fuck, fuck. I can barely breathe.

'Wondering what?' I manage to croak out.

'Wondering who or what you really are. And then, I remembered.'

'Remembered what?' The words almost don't make it past my lips.

'I remembered that the night Cassie died, when I came home from work and checked on her, there was no water bottle beside her bed. I realised then that you lied about when you brought her the water bottle, which means that at some stage during the night you spent some time in Cassie's room and for some reason you wanted no one to know about it.'

I sob silently. Huge salt drops fall onto my clenched hands. For the first time that I can remember, my tears are real. I am crying for lost opportunities, for things I might have done, people I might have been. I am crying for the fact that for the first time ever I have been fully revealed. I am crying because my husband has constructed a prison for me. It is a prison built on knowledge and power. It is a prison that may be strong enough to contain even me.

Daniel walks over to me and places one arm around my shoulders. It is a magnanimous gesture, that of a conquering hero showing his captive some kindness.

'Do you want to know what I've decided?'

I nod. It is impossible for me to speak.

'I thought about what is important to me, about what might be able to be saved out of all this, and I decided that the only thing I can really do is to make sure that my family is not destroyed any further. It's the only thing I have left to cling to. I expect Zach to be raised in a way that is the best for him. I will have nothing denied to my only surviving child, *our* son. Do you understand what I'm asking of you?'

Of course I understand. I am to subjugate myself to the needs of the family; I am to return to the role of being Zach's mother, Daniel's wife. Daniel's knowledge has granted him the right to demand this of me and I do the only thing I am capable of: I nod again.

Daniel removes his arm. 'Come on, let's keep walking.'

He swings the pack up onto his shoulders and sets off. I follow, even though I am unable to control the shaking in my knees. Bile rises in my throat and I must swallow constantly to keep from vomiting. All my negotiating power has been removed and we both know it. For the first time ever, someone, Daniel, understands me, fully and completely. My future has been defined, decided, limited. I have been stripped bare, pegged and laid out in the sun to dry.

Daniel's pace is quicker than it was before. I struggle to keep up. The clouds have broken; sun slants into the valley. The flies become heavier, the heat more oppressive. I move as if through a thick fog.

Soon we begin our ascent to the viewing platform. Loose stones, dislodged by Daniel's feet, sometimes roll onto my head and hands. Once, a rock comes off in my hand and in the cool, red earth beneath I see a centipede. Its glossy back shines iridescent in the sunlight. Carefully I replace the rock.

At a particularly steep point Daniel turns back and offers me his hand. I take it gratefully. His steadiness emphasises the trembling in my own limbs.

We reach the summit and, as promised, a semi-circle of flat earth about ten metres long and six metres deep constitutes the viewing platform. Daniel and I stand for a few moments, the silence broken only by the sound of our breathing.

Ahead of us are the five pillars, splendid in the noon sunlight, rising defiantly from the valley floor far below. They look like carefully arranged layers of loose shale, as if some giant child has constructed a play city. But their almost fragile appearance belies the fact that they are the only remains of the material that once stood all around them. They alone have been able to withstand millions of years of weathering. Far below, at the base of the pillars, is the forest: green in their shadow, shimmering blue-green in the distance. It is as if we are the only creatures alive up here; it is as if we own the Earth. I know why the devil chose a hilltop upon which to offer Jesus his greatest temptation.

I am standing as close to the edge as I comfortably can. Heights have never been my strong point, but even from where I am, I can see that the viewing platform is actually a ledge. We are suspended in a gravity-defying time and space. One day this ledge will break away and tumble into the valley below. I picture it, somersaulting over and over until it crashes against the trees and pulverises into a cloud of lung-choking dust.

Daniel has walked past me, beyond me; he stops only when he is standing on the very edge of the world.

I look at Daniel, his silhouette superimposed on the almost impenetrable bush that stretches below and beyond us for kilometres. If someone fell from this ledge his or her body would probably never be found. I wonder for a moment what Daniel is doing. Is he challenging me? Or is he offering himself to me? He has just uttered the words that will circumscribe my life, and yet he is standing before me as if he is unknowing, as if he is deliberately offering me what is now perhaps *my* greatest temptation.

And then, with a great rush of clarity, I realise the truth. Daniel doesn't know me at all. He has no inkling of what I am capable. Oh, he may think he does, but the truth he has grasped hold of is merely a shadow truth, merely a small glimpse of the power and ruthlessness that live at my centre.

Daniel is guileless, a simpleton, offering himself to me in that way. I feel almost giddy with the thought of the endless possibilities opening before me, and the enormous temptation that he is presenting to me. I move closer. The dry dirt crunches under my feet.

Daniel turns his head to look at me. In his grey eyes I see myself reflected, reflected as I have always been. It was this way when we first met. I had believed then that it was the stillness of his gaze that would grant me my uniqueness, now I knew better.

I stop in my forward movement and regard him. I realise that I will go no further. It would be too easy. This is not, after all, how I want it to be. There will be other edges, other times. There is strength in knowing your power and yet holding back.

And then, the moment is lost; Daniel moves away from the edge and we begin the downhill trek.

That night Daniel is a man whose shackles have been removed. He is gayer than I have seen him in a long time. His shoulders have straightened and his steps have lightened. He believes he has played his trump card and won.

If he expects me to be morose, however, then he is mistaken. I act the woman who has surrendered gracefully to her fate. I act the compliant wife, the demure mother. My demeanour is the unruffled sheet that covers the writhing nest of vipers.

Later we fuck.

Every pore in my body is hot and Daniel meets me with his own fire. I seek out every way I know of amplifying my own pleasure and Daniel seems happy to acquiesce. He believes, after all, that he has won. Why shouldn't he satisfy me in this at least. He works hard and yet I hold myself back. It is only when his head is firmly buried between my wet thighs that I allow myself to come in a great shuddering gasp that shakes the room with its assumed surrender.

TWENTY-FIVE

We are home. It has been a long trip, much of it travelled in silence. I drove while Daniel slept. I didn't mind; after all, I don't have to work tomorrow. Anyway, I didn't need Daniel's conversation to keep me awake; I was surging on adrenaline. I found a radio station playing dance music. It pounded out a rhythm that thumped in time with my heart. I pumped the accelerator to the beat. I felt good. As we entered the city it began to rain. I kept the windscreen wipers on high and opened the window a sliver. The fresh blast of cooling afternoon air did me good. I felt as if I could go on forever.

Now, at home, I am making a final cup of coffee for Mother before her departure when I realise there is no milk in the fridge. Daniel says he will go out and buy some as I have done most of the driving today. It is a simple offer by him, one which in the past I would have accepted without a second thought. Once I acted instinctively, out of habit, or indifference or desperation. But now I have changed. Now I know – every action has a reaction and in every offer there is an opportunity. And so, I agree to Daniel's suggestion and at the same time ask if he will take my car and check the tyre pressure. It's a bit of a nuisance for him as he will have to move his car from where it's parked behind mine in the garage, but it's a job I don't like to do and one that he normally does for me.

When Daniel leaves I make my way down the hallway to begin unpacking. As I pass the internal entrance to the garage I notice that, as I have expected, Daniel has left the garage door open. He often does this when he slips out for a short while, and today in particular, he would not want to get out of the car in the rain to open the garage door when he returns. Our house sits on a slight rise; you cannot see into the garage until you are right at its entrance.

Zach is pushing his pedal-less trike around the house. It was a gift from Daniel's parents for his first birthday. He has only recently started to use it and his feet barely touch the ground. After a short time I can't stand the noise of Zach pushing up and down the corridor. It is still raining and I suggest to Mother that she take Zach into the garage. He has plenty of space to ride in there and she can supervise him while I unpack. If nothing else, it will kill two birds with the one stone: remove the need to talk to my mother and deal with Zach's noise.

I return to my unpacking. In the new silence of the house I begin to hum. It is a tune of my own creation, rising and falling, speeding up and slowing down with complete unpredictability. It pleases me, this unfettered melody that needs to satisfy no one but myself.

When I have finished unpacking, I head down the corridor towards the garage in order to store the suitcase. It is then that I hear the sound of my car, driven by Daniel, beginning to accelerate up the drive. He knows that the garage door is open, waiting for him, and he drives quickly to avoid the bother of changing gears. It is how he usually drives up the rise to our house. I have told him before that he comes much too fast up the hill.

I can see my mother's back as she sits on the floor by the internal door to the garage. She is leaning against the door jamb nonchalantly flicking through a magazine. She is as predictable in her habits as Daniel, and as usual she is not watching Zach properly. I have warned Daniel many times that my mother cannot be trusted. I have told him how much I despise her. Perhaps after this people will listen more closely to what I have to say.

I am not far enough along the corridor to see directly into the garage, but as I hear Daniel speed to the top of the drive, I can imagine Zach caught like a startled rabbit in the glare of his headlights. I know that in such a situation split-second reactions mean the difference between life and death. I know that in my car the pedals are further apart and higher up than they are in Daniel's. Daniel does not often drive my car, and I wonder: will he be able to find the brake in time?

It is only now that I allow myself to picture a scene in the future. Senior Constable Coombs has re-entered our lives. This time she is questioning Daniel. He sits on the couch with his arms pulled tight over his chest. He looks like a man whose soul has been removed. I imagine that his eyes have sunk into his face. They have lost their reflective quality. Perhaps they have even changed colour. He looks at me and I know that, finally, he understands me. But now I am strong enough that I no longer care.

In my imaginings I also respond to police inquiries. This time, however, I am not afraid of what they may ask; I am not concerned that my reactions will be inappropriate. I have had practice, you see; I am better at this than ever before. This time I will be prepared to help the police. I will honestly answer the questions they ask me about Daniel. I will show them the note I wrote all those months ago, the written word which proves how Cassie really died.

But for now I wait, I wait to see. Will Daniel find the brake in time or won't he?

EPILOGUE

*T*here are very few things I have taken with me. Even most of the memories have been discarded. Memories are burdensome things, almost as bad as names, and if you think I care at all about what happened to those I left behind, then you are mistaken.

There is, however, one possession from that time which I cherish, one which I keep with me. It is the twisted Möbius strip, which lies nestled and safe in its velvet-lined box. It is not for sentimental reasons that I maintain this one possession. True, it was given to me by a man I once thought I loved; a man who regarded the gift as a symbol of two entities becoming one. For a time I had believed him, but now, after all that I have survived, I know better. Now I know that *I* am the Möbius strip. *I* am the self-contained entity needing no one and nothing to make myself complete. This is the only knowledge I will ever need. And it is the Möbius strip which serves to remind me.

And now perhaps you wonder, where am I, what has become of me? And I laugh at that wondering, because in that question I sense some fear. Does it trouble you that one day I may reappear, perhaps as your neighbour, your lover, your friend?

Anything, of course, is possible. And you may have good cause for fear...

ACKNOWLEDGEMENTS

When I first started writing *The Mother's Tale* – in small amounts of private, stolen time – I had no idea how collaborative its path to publication would ultimately become.

I didn't know that I, and my book, would need the help of people of all sorts: those to believe in us and cheer us along; those to provide an opportunity when some doors seemed to be firmly closed; those whose skills in editing, or promotion or marketing, no good book or author can be without.

There is first and foremost my husband. My one-man cheer squad, who believes I can do absolutely anything I set my mind to. There are so many things he did, but just as important are the things he didn't do. He didn't push me to get a real job when our youngest child started school, he didn't complain when beds weren't made, floors not swept, windows not cleaned (even when I had been at home all day and appeared to have done nothing at all with my time). He didn't complain when for many weeks, he acted as a single dad while I wrote. *The Mother's Tale* would not be without him – so to my husband with all my love, thank you.

And then there are my children, my great levellers, who also put up with all of the above but who, if I became too stressed about something, would bring me down to earth with statements like 'But Mum it's only a book'. Not nearly as important as when dinner was going to be served and how the arrangements for their birthday parties were progressing, and nor should it be! Thank you my children, you are my reality; solid and unbelievably wonderful.

To my extended family and friends who gave me support every step of the way (including child-minding, dog walking and dinners for my family when I was away). It is a tribute to them all that I can think of no negative comment I have *ever* received about the path I was pursuing. And believe me that is no small thing, when the journey often seems so long and the outcome so uncertain! Thank you all for your love and encouragement.

Taking *The Mother's Tale* beyond my tight network of family and friends was a big step. And I have no doubt that its path to publication would have been much, much harder without the help of one amazing person and one completely unique foundation. I am talking about Peter Bishop, the creative director of Varuna – the Writers' House – administered by the Eleanor Dark Foundation (Varuna was gifted to the foundation by Eleanor's son, Mr Michael Dark). Peter and Varuna are unique in Australia (and possibly the world). They provide a link between writing as a solitary pursuit and writing which is part of a wider community of fellow practitioners, publishers and readers.

Peter was the first 'outside' reader of *The Mother's Tale* and his insightful comments, ongoing support and enthusiasm, combined with a couple of residencies at Varuna, resulted in a work which I felt confident in taking to the broader world of publishers and agents. To Peter and Varuna, I don't think you will ever know how eternally grateful I am.

A big, heartfelt thank you to Pippa Masson, my agent, who believed in *The Mother's Tale* from the very early days – still evolving as it then was. Every writer needs a good agent and Pippa is one of the best. Enthusiastic, responsive and professional!

To my publisher: the full-spirited, amazing Vanessa Radnidge at Hachette Livre. Not only does she have an eye for a good book, but she is so wonderfully up-beat, highly intelligent and a pleasure to work with. Vanessa saw *The Mother's Tale* at a reasonably early stage of its development and believed in it from the start. Thanks for everything Vanessa!

Thank you also to Amanda O'Connell and Deonie Fiford, who did the final editing fine-tune (which resulted in improvements to *The Mother's Tale* even at the eleventh hour!). I cannot express what a relief it was for me to have the two of you to help hone some of the finer points of my novel.

Now to the Orion marketing and publicity teams led by Sandy Weir and Emma Noble. What a professional group of people! Again it is your capability and enthusiasm which shines through. I feel so lucky to have had *The Mother's Tale* in your talented hands for the final stages of its development.

Camilla Noli, 2008

The
Mother's Tale
CAMILLA NOLI

Introduction to *The Mother's Tale*

What lies beneath . . .

Hidden fears, intimate secrets, dark motivations.

From the warm light of her sleeping baby's nursery, the curve of her husband's arm, the soft embrace of an old friend, the anonymous narrator of *The Mother's Tale* whispers to you her private fears, her deepest held desires.

Mesmerising, confronting, revealing, her hidden secrets are a distorted echo of the emotions of every-woman: mother, lover, friend, daughter.

From its softly lit beginning to its explosive, emotional conclusion *The Mother's Tale* takes the reader on a journey to the dark recesses of one woman's heart and mind; within are the truths that are not spoken, the realities that are not written about.

The Mother's Tale is a taut, beautifully con-structed book which, once begun, cannot be put down, told by a narrator who will not be forgotten easily. It engages and confronts; it provokes.

About the author

Camilla Noli lives on the Central Coast of New South Wales with her husband and two children. *The Mother's Tale* is her first novel. She is currently working on her next book.

If you visit Camilla's iLounge (www.camilla noli.com) you will find links to her discussion board with online debate, a range of her short stories, news and information about Camilla, and some useful information and links for readers and writers.

Camilla Noli on writing

I have been a writer for a very long time – long before I was published in any form whatsoever.

I never gave up my dream of being a published author, but along the way I completed two degrees [BA (Hons) in Literature and an MBA], I travelled, worked, got married, worked a bit more, and gave birth to two wonderful children. During this time I never stopped writing.

In the very early days, writing was my way of working out the world. As a child I would write down those things that worried me, moved me, disturbed me. Often these writings were in narrative form, sometimes they were fictionalised. I vividly recall writing one piece from the point of view of a foetus who was just about to be aborted. Not long before, I had seen a picture of Edvard Munch's classic painting *The Scream* and I remember that his work was very firmly in my mind as I wrote.

Another short story that I wrote in primary school was entitled *The Girl Who Loved Apples*. The protagonist of this story, a primary school girl, loved apples so much that she would do anything to find the perfect source of her favourite fruit. One day in the park, she met a kindred soul, an old man who possessed the source of the perfect apple – a tree in the garden surrounding his ramshackle house. The story ended with the girl going to live with the man so that she could have constant access to the tree. In my story the two of them, young girl and old man, were perfectly happy with the arrangement. Following her desires seemed to me to be a much more interesting story than if the girl had given them up in order to be a 'good daughter'.

Exploration of the concept that Jung called the 'shadow', or what could simply be called our dark side – those repressed desires and impulses that most of us work so hard to hide and which are actually so important in understanding our motivations – is a large part of what has driven my work to date.

Writing is still my method for working out the world and for fully developing and exploring ideas. It's just that now some of the things I want to explore are more serious and complicated than they once were. The other difference, of course, is that now I am published I can look forward to other people reading and discussing some of the ideas that fascinate me.

The background to *The Mother's Tale*

In 2001, I began writing the book that would become *The Mother's Tale*. From the very first, it was the intriguing character of the narrator that captured me. My anonymous narrator carried me along and the majority of the book was written very quickly. By 2002 I had a book which I knew was nearly, but not quite, right.

In 2003 I was lucky enough to be chosen to attend a manuscript development program run by Peter Bishop at Varuna – the Writers' House in the

Blue Mountains. With Peter's insightful reading and comment on the novel, it developed further – to the extent that in 2004 I was the recipient of a Varuna/HarperCollins Award for manuscript development. This was a 10-day residential program where I, and four other writers, were given the opportunity to work with an editor from HarperCollins who had chosen our manuscript as being a work which they wanted to help develop further.

What an amazing experience that was! It was the first time I had been exposed to the workings of the publishing world and doing so in the environs of a place like Varuna, with an editor who truly loved my work, was surreal. *The Mother's Tale* developed further under that editorial direction.

Towards the end of 2004 I began my second novel. This book also benefited from the reading and feedback it received from Peter Bishop. In mid-2006, with two as yet unpublished novels under my belt, I was lucky enough to have Pippa Masson at Curtis Brown Literary Agents agree to represent me as my agent. Early in 2007 I learnt that *The Mother's Tale* would be published in 2008 by Hachette Livre, with another novel to follow in 2009.

Q&A with Camilla Noli

Q: How did you come up with the idea for *The Mother's Tale*?

The Mother's Tale is a book which is driven entirely by its strong central character and first person narrator. The personality of this character presented itself to me almost fully formed one night and from the very beginning she fascinated me.

What would it be like to be inside the mind of someone like her, I wondered? More importantly, what would happen if someone like her had responsibility for very young, vulnerable children, and if she were placed in situations which for her were increasingly stressful? It didn't take long for both this character and these scenarios to absorb my thinking, and so *The Mother's Tale* was born. In a sense I felt as if I *had* to create a story for this person.

People who have read the book have told me that the narrator's character is one which they also find difficult to get out of their mind. Mothers have told me that, often to their horror, they realise they have moments in their lives when they find themselves thinking and acting (in small ways!) as she does. The truth is that we all have times in our lives when we 'act' things out, when there is a disconnection between what we think and what we say. But the narrator of *The Mother's Tale* is a full-time performer – all her life is an act, and so she becomes an increasingly fascinating person as we almost, but not quite, come to understand her.

This fascination with strong, often unpleasant, unusual or unhappy characters is something that recurs in my work. One of my short stories – which you can find if you visit my iLounge – is called *Groom or no Groom*. Once again this story grew from a dream of a very intriguing main character, who practically demanded that a story be written for her.

In fact, in my opinion the best stories all have very strong, unforgettable characters at their centre.

Q: **Many people find the idea behind *The Mother's Tale* quite disturbing. Did you ever find it difficult to write?**

The ideas at the centre of *The Mother's Tale* are disturbing. But I do believe that they are ideas that need to be talked about, and highlighting certain issues within a fictional context is a perfect way for opening debate on them.

Interestingly, the most disturbing parts of *The Mother's Tale* were written very quickly, driven by very powerful emotion – a kind of suspended horror – at what the words were saying. I suspect that it was necessary for me to construct these scenes in a rush or they wouldn't, or couldn't, be written at all.

In fact those more disturbing parts of *The Mother's Tale*, written in a burst of emotion, are the ones which have changed least over my many years of working on the novel. I have found this both before and since with my writing. Scenes written with a very strong emotional content seem to flow, as if every word knows where it needs to be.

And as disturbing as some of the ideas and scenes within *The Mother's Tale* are, they are absolutely central to understanding the personality of the main character and for exploring the issues which are at the heart of the novel.

Q: What kind of response do you hope readers will have to *The Mother's Tale*?

Well, of course I hope that readers will love it! And I hope that it makes people think. I hope that it provokes debate.

I think that all the best books are capable of generating a conversation around themselves; they have a life beyond their covers. These are books which you just have to talk about with your partner, or your best friend, or the person sitting beside you on the train. This 'desire to discuss' is what the best books do and I hope that *The Mother's Tale* does that as well.

Already, different people have had vastly different responses to *The Mother's Tale*, often depending on their own experiences and background. And that's a good thing! I hope that people do want to discuss *The Mother's Tale* and its issues. If the book achieves that then it will have done as much as I could have hoped for.

Q: What research did you do for the book?

The Mother's Tale reflects preoccupations I have had for many years and in this sense, much of the 'research', particularly with regard to the personality of the main character, was carried out prior to writing the novel. Because the novel takes such an intensely personal point of view, once the character of the narrator was firmly established, large slabs of the book were written with me simply making sure that I stayed fully inside her head.

I did, however, carry out specific research with regard to some of the more technical aspects of the book. And I don't really want to say more than that, in case you are reading this before having read the book!

Q: What do you think of reading groups?

Books shouldn't exist in isolation, they should be shared and the best of them should be capable of acting as springboards to a whole range of emotions, and topics for discussion. I believe that a good reading group provides a purpose-built mechanism for that to happen.

Personally, as well as being a writer I am also an avid reader and a member of a number of formal and informal book clubs. I love receiving book recommendations from friends and I love having the opportunity to discuss thought provoking books with other like-minded readers. It is truly one of the great joys of my life!

Q: Who are some of your favourite writers?

I read widely and voraciously and it is very difficultfor me to pick out only a few favourite writers as I enjoy a wide variety for different reasons – but I will try!

I have spent many years enjoying the South American magic realist writers such as Gabriel Garcia Márquez, Jorge Borges and Isabel Allende. I also love the metafictional works of people like Umberto Eco.

As a child I enjoyed Agatha Christie. Her ability to show the dark side of seemingly idyllic English villages and lives, still fascinates me. At his best, Stephen King has a similar ability – the exploration of seemingly normal lives pulled apart by sinister events or dark impulses.

I still enjoy good detective fiction – writers such as Gabrielle Lord, Ian Rankin, Lisa Gardner and many others.

At university I studied a range of Australian authors with my Honour's thesis being written on Peter Carey's *Illywhacker*. At the time I found his work to be a breath of fresh air and I have continued reading many Australian authors including Kate Grenville, Tim Winton, Helen Garner, Gail Jones, Patrick White and Janette Turner Hospital (whose writing I truly admire), to name a few. We have an enormous depth of talent in Australia and my shortlist has merely scratched the surface.

It is always a delight to discover fiction which is truly imaginative. Books which fall into this category for me include *Life of Pi* (Yann Martel), *Perfume* (Patrick Suskind), *The Raw Shark Texts* (Steven Hall) and anything by Haruki Murakami.

There are also books which I have enjoyed for the sheer beauty of their writing. Novels such as Shirley Hazzard's *The Great Fire*, Ian McEwan's *Atonement* and Cormac McCarthy's *The Road* can be savoured for almost their every word.

Finally, my list would not have even scratched the surface without mentioning: A.S. Byatt, John Fowles, John Irving and Margaret Atwood.

And believe me that is just the beginning!

Q: You've just finished writing your second book, how did the experience compare to the first?

Unfortunately it doesn't become any easier!

I believe there are two truly amazing points when writing a novel. The first comes when you are visited by the original idea. It is an idea which seems entirely unique and which must be explored. It is an idea which you believe can sustain your interest as a writer (and your readers' interest).

Reading group questions for
The Mother's Tale

The Mother's Tale is a provoking, unconventional novel daring to explore one of society's last great taboos – the idea that there are some women who are quite simply neither naturally maternal nor nurturing. Below are some questions which could be used as starting points for your reading group's discussion of some of the topical issues raised by *The Mother's Tale*.

1. The narrator of *The Mother's Tale* remains unnamed throughout the novel. Why do you think the author has chosen to do this? Do you think it is a successful device and if so, how and why?

2. *The Mother's Tale* breaks from convention in the fact that its narrator is not an immediately warm or likeable woman. At any stage during the reading of *The Mother's Tale* did you find yourself feeling sympathetic towards its narrator? If so, when did you lose sympathy for her? Did your sympathy return at any point?

3. The narrator provides the reader with a graphic description of the birth of her first child and its aftermath, where she had trouble bonding with the baby. In your opinion do you think this failure to bond can be seen as explaining any of her subsequent actions? Do you believe that the narrator's behaviour could be attributable to postpartum depression? Why or why not?

4. Do you think the hospital should or could have been more vigilant in picking up and addressing the narrator's ambivalence towards Cassie at the time of her birth? Do you think this would have made any difference to her subsequent actions?
   - What is your experience of, and views on, the postnatal care provided by hospitals and child-health clinics?
   - What is your experience of, and views on, the support provided in our society to families in general?

5. The narrator's husband, Daniel, is an important character in *The Mother's Tale*. To what extent do you think his actions can be seen as being either a contributing or driving factor behind the

narrator's actions and responses throughout the novel?

- Do you think Daniel should bear any of the responsibility for what happens in the novel?

6. The narrator claims that her relationship with Daniel is similar to that between herself and her father. Do you see similarities in the relationships, particularly when taking the roles of the narrator's mother and daughter into account? Do you see differences?

7. The narrator partly blames her mother for the lack of confidence which she experiences in her own mothering abilities. Do you think this is true?

- Do you believe that the mothering instinct is innate, or do you think it has to be learned?

8. One of the images used in *The Mother's Tale* is of a Möbius strip. In what way do you see the

A Möbius strip is a mathematical construct which can be made by taking a flat band of material, giving it a half twist and then joining it. The resulting structure has only one side and one surface. Sometimes known as the 'eternity symbol', the Möbius strip has fascinated artists and writers since its discovery in 1858. M.C. Escher, amongst others, has used it as the basis for a number of his etched images.

image of the Möbius strip as being important to
the novel? You may wish to consider this question
with regard to both the nature of the narrator
and the structure of the book.

9. *The Mother's Tale* is a self-contained novel told
from the point of view of the narrator and main
character. To what extent do you think her story
can be fully believed? Are there any points in
the novel where you feel the narrator's authority
as storyteller, and ultimate source of truth for
the novel, is undermined? How would any such
undermining affect your reading of the novel?

10. What do you think has become of the narrator
by the end of *The Mother's Tale*? Do you think
it is important that the reader knows from where
the narrator last speaks?

11. One of the books which the author says influ-
enced the writing of *The Mother's Tale* is Dr
Robert Hare's book *Without Conscience: The
Disturbing World of the Psychopaths Among
Us*. In this book Dr Hare describes a psychopath
as: someone who is capable of 'using their charm

and chameleon-like abilities to cut a wide swath through society and leaving a wake of ruined lives behind them'. A person 'lacking in empathy and the ability to form warm emotional relationships with others . . . who functions without conscience'. To what extent do you view the narrator of *The Mother's Tale* as exhibiting psychopathiclike qualities? To what extent do you think she is simply highly narcissistic?